REV. FRANCIS R. DAVIS
ST. PATRICK'S CHURCH
274 DENISON PKWY. E.
CORNING, NEW YORK 14830-2995

NO SLOUCH

NO SLOUCH

by

Tom McDevitt

LITTLE RED HEN, INC.
Post Office Box 4260   Pocatello, Idaho 83201

This is book number _____ of a
limited first printing of 1000.

Copyright © 1979 by Tom McDevitt

First printing

Library of Congress Catalog Card No. 78-70914

ISBN-0-933046-00-6 Hard $8.95

All rights reserved. No part of this book may be reproduced in any form or by any electronic or mechanical means including information storage and retrieval systems without permission in writing from the publisher, except by a reviewer who may quote brief passages in a review.

TO
LITTLE RED

The characters and incidents in this novel are wholly fictional. Any similarity to persons or happenings in real life is coincidental.

NO SLOUCH

CHAPTER I

Billy and I were standing on the sidewalk in front of Nick's Place when the two squaws came out the side door into the alley. The short fat squaw was first. She tripped, caught herself, then leaned heavily against the wall. Her faded blue cotton dress split two inches at the sides.

The big fat squaw stuck her head out of the door, caught sight of the woman leaning against the wall, and let fly with a beer bottle. She missed. The bottle hit the gravel, bounced twice, then broke. "Son-a-bitch," she mumbled. Little Fat Squaw grabbed a handful of rocks and flung them at the door. She too missed. The head had popped back inside. "Yogo!" she said.

Billy stood wide eyed and staring. He was only twelve. I laughed. I was sixteen. "Yogo." I whispered the Shoshone word for screw under my breath.

Big Fat Squaw came stumbling out into the alley. She

had been pushed. Several Indian men and two other women stepped out behind her.

Little Fat Squaw grabbed another handful of gravel and heaved them at the bigger woman. This time she didn't miss. Big Fat Squaw yelled in pain as the rocks struck her in the chest. Her faded pink cotton dress tore an inch down the middle. "Son-a-bitch," she said again, and came at Little Fat Squaw.

For a while the two women faced each other spitting and trying to scratch eyes. Then Big Fat Squaw hooked a hand into Little Fat Squaw's hair, jerked the smaller woman off balance and slammed her against the wall.

The male spectators laughed. One of the women spectators cheered, the other cursed and jerked a man's hand from the top of her dress. "Wow!" said Billy. He meant the fight.

"Wow!" I said. I meant the hand in the dress.

Little Fat Squaw tried to get up but couldn't. She slumped down under a kick from Big Fat Squaw's tennis shoes. She turned in the gravel with her face to the wall and yelled. "Help! Help!"

The spectators and Big Fat Squaw laughed. Billy started after the woman. I jerked him back. Big Fat Squaw continued to kick. Her dress split another inch down the middle.

Little Fat Squaw quit yelling, rolled over on her back and caught the tennis shoe. Big Fat Squaw flopped on her butt.

Little Fat Squaw rolled on top of the bigger woman, knocked her flat, then sunk her teeth into the brown flesh protruding through the split in Big Fat Squaw's dress.

Big Fat Squaw screamed in agony. The men and one woman spectator cheered. The other woman spectator cursed and jerked a male hand from beneath her dress. "Wow!" said Billy. "Wow!" I repeated.

Big Fat Squaw bucked and twisted, but couldn't dislodge the terrier. A rivlet of blood trickled into her navel. The dress split another inch. She was wearing white panties. "Son-a-bitch," she said and reached for some rocks. Her hand touched a piece of the broken beer bottle. She grabbed it and thrust it at the face buried in her abdomen.

10

The jagged glass caught Little Fat Squaw in the left eye. The littler woman let off her biting, screamed and rolled over clutching her face. Big Fat Squaw still holding the bottle, grunted, got to her feet and looked down at the other woman. "Son-a-bitch," she said, then sat on Little Fat Squaw's chest and cut her eye out.

"Oh my God!" Billy got sick and vomitted in the gutter. I didn't feel too good myself. The spectators and Big Fat Squaw went back inside Nick's Place. Little Fat Squaw lay writhing in the alley.

"We've got to do something." Billy had recovered a little.

"We don't have to," I said. A squad car came down the alley. The Pocatello police drove white Pontiac Le Mans. Two policemen got out. They tried to help Little Fat Squaw but she was screaming and carrying on so much they had to handcuff her hands behind her back before they could put a bandage on her eye and get her into the back of the prowl car.

"This is something new," said one policeman.

"Yeah," agreed the other. He closed his eyes and shuddered. "Geesus!"

"You stay here with her," said the first policeman. "I'll go inside and see what this mess is all about." He stepped in the side door of the bar.

In a minute he came outside with Nick. Nick Podakas was a squirrel headed little Greek; shiny bald and with a walrus moustache. Nick looked malevolently at Billy and I. He didn't like kids hanging around. "Gives the place a bad name," he said.

"What you know about this?" The policeman pointed at the squaw.

"Nothing," said Nick. He glanced again at Billy and me, then went back inside.

The policeman came up to us, tossled my hair, then put his hand on Billy's shoulder. "What do the McGrath boys know about this?" he asked. Pocatello is a red neck town of forty thousand and people pretty much know each other.

"Nothing," I said.

The policeman grinned. "Is that so?" He looked at Billy.

"The big fat squaw did it," said Billy. "The one with the torn dress. Sat on her and cut her eye out with a beer bottle!" The telling of it made him sick again and he vomitted.

The policeman patted Billy on the back, then went into the bar and came out with Big Fat Squaw. They handcuffed her and put her next to Little Fat Squaw in the back seat. "Son-a-bitch," she said. The prowl car went into the street and turned toward the hospital.

"What we gonna do now?" asked Billy. He'd recovered pretty good from watching the fight.

"I thought we'd go for a shake," I said.

"You got any money?" Billy eyed me suspiciously.

"No," I said. "I'm temporarily impecunious." I liked to use big words.

"Then we ain't going after any shakes," said Billy.

"You got some!" I accused him. Billy was a hard working little guy and always had money.

"Right and I'm keeping it," he said.

"Tightwad! I ought to lean on you hard," I said. "Like smash your teeth in."

"Try it!" Billy said. "Just try it!"

I didn't. Not because I couldn't take him, because I could real easy. I was pretty big even then, being five ten and bigger by a head than Dad. And Billy was short, not even five feet.

But the trouble with Billy was, he'd never quit. You'd punch him and punch him and he'd keep coming. Then you'd get scared, thinking you'd really hurt him, but he didn't care and he'd keep swinging at you, and sometimes he'd connect and that would hurt too. So I didn't fight with Billy over the money.

From inside the bar we could hear yelling. I went to the door and peeked inside. Buddy Bearpaw was arguing with Nick about credit. Nick didn't give any, and Buddy Bearpaw was broke. Nick Podakas was five feet tall and a hundred pounds. Buddy Bearpaw was six feet two inches and two hundred-fifty pounds. The yelling got pretty strong and I could see that Buddy Bearpaw wanted to reach across and grab Nick, only he knew better. Behind the bar the Greek had an axe handle that could lay a man's head open. He'd done that. He also had a .357 magnum that could blow a man's head off. He'd done that too.

After awhile Buddy Bearpaw staggered out to where Billy and I were. I'll tell you about Buddy Bearpaw.

Buddy Bearpaw was a Shoshone Indian who lived on the Fort Hall Indian Reservation seven miles north of Pocatello. He'd been plenty smart as a kid and had gone through high school and then onto college. Also he could cowboy better than most anyone in the world. And he didn't do the safe stuff either, like calf roping. Buddy Bearpaw rode the bareback broncs, and the bulls, and the rest of that crippling stuff, and he made the rodeo circuit, and went to the Nationals. Then for a while no one heard anything about him, until one day he showed back up in town a drunken bum. He never rode, he never worked, he never done anything, only drink and cause trouble.

Like I said Buddy Bearpaw was a big guy and he had lots of black hair that wasn't too long, but kept flopping in his face anyway. He was supposed to have one of those hooked Indian noses, but it had been broken so many times it wandered all over his face. Also he had fat lips that were purple from drinking.

Buddy Bearpaw wore a red plaid shirt with the fourth button missing where his brown belly hung out and he wore Levis, his championship rodeo buckle, and brown cowboy boots that didn't have any manure on them.

"Hey kid, you got money?" Buddy Bearpaw grabbed Billy's arm.

"Sure," said Billy. He smiled up at Buddy Bearpaw. Billy liked the Indian guy. That's how crazy my little brother was.

"Give it to me." Buddy Bearpaw was surprised. It had been a long time since someone had admitted to him that they had money.

"I'll lend you half," said Billy. He shoved his hand in a pocket and came up with a dollar bill.

"Thanks!" Buddy Bearpaw made a grab for the bill.

"Now just a minute!" I stepped forward. "You give that money back!" I grabbed Buddy Bearpaw's arm. That was a mistake. He caught me under the left eye and I went down.

For a minute everything was black, then things came around and I saw Buddy Bearpaw going back inside the bar.

"Wow! He sure leaned on you!" Billy was staring down at me.

I tried to get up but couldn't. Billy offered me his hand. I slapped it. "Get away from me, you Judas," I said.

That stung. Billy started to cry. "I didn't mean to cause any trouble, Davy," he said. "I never would have done it if I thought you would get hurt. You know that."

I knew it and got to my feet. "Let's go home."

"You gonna get him?" asked Billy when we were away from Nick's.

"No," I said. "People who seek revenge are stupid. It's never worth it. I'll get even if I get the chance, but I'm not going out of my way to prove anything to a jerk like that."

"That's smart," said Billy. He only agreed because he was afraid that if I went after Buddy Bearpaw I'd end up on the ground again, or even worse.

We went down Center Street. A half block ahead an old guy in dirty overalls and scuffed boots shuffled out one bar, then into the one next door. "There goes Zane Bodkins," I said.

"Acts like he didn't see us," said Billy.

"He sees plenty," I said. I'll tell you about Zane Bodkins.

The Bodkins boys, Zane's father and uncle, came up from Utah in 1908, which was about the time the Indians sold part of the reservation. The brothers and their wives homesteaded a section of land just south of town.

The land was poor. Some years it grew a crop; some years it didn't. But the Bodkins stuck it out until hard work and poverty took its inevitable toll. The elders died and Zane being the only child, inherited all 640 acres.

Zane learned a lesson from his parents, he never let hard work kill him. Fact is, he didn't do any work, hard or otherwise. He ran a dozen scrawny cows on the place. Sold off the calves in the fall, and boozed until the money was gone.

When younger, Zane was married long enough to father a boy, then his wife took the child and moved out of the shack Zane had on his place. Unlike Zane, she and the boy couldn't subsist on cheap whiskey.

Zane stayed on his place until his shack burned down, then he moved into an abandoned homesteader's cottage on our ranch, only we didn't own it then, the Judge did. Cause Zane didn't bother nobody, nothing was ever said.

Well, the town grew, and Zane's bad land place started to look better everyday. One day his grown and married son decided it was time that dear old pappy come live with his family.

Zane resisted the invitation for several years but finally gave in and moved to his son's house. In a short time the son and the bank had the ranch.

Zane stayed at his son's house a while longer. To his credit, despite all pressures of family and church, not once did the old man waver from his life's pattern. The few thousand he got for the farm, he used to buy booze, and bail his Indian girlfriend out of jail.

Then late one night his daughter-in-law caught a drunken Zane out in the garage laying a squaw over the hood of his rattle trap car. Bounced from the family nest, Zane retired to the sanctuary of his cottage on our ranch.

We looked in and waved at Zane standing at the bar, but he still acted like he didn't see us.

We got to South Baker Street and cut across Harold's Conoco station on the corner. A fat greasy attendant waved at Billy. "Who is that?" I asked.

"That's Coot," said Billy. "Him and me are building a stock car!"

"Hah!" I said. "That ought to be something." It would be two years before Billy could drive during daylight hours and probably another four before he could drive a stock car. "That thing'll be rusted out before you ever get behind the wheel."

"You'll see," said Billy. He didn't like me laughing at him and his friend, Coot.

"We're gonna be home on time for a change," said Billy.

"Yeah!" I said. My eye had swelled shut. I reached up and touched it.

"Dad's gonna wonder about that eye. He doesn't like us going to Nick's Place. What you gonna tell him?"

"I'll think of something," I said. "You gonna squeal?"

"No," said Billy. He meant it too. When he'd promised something Billy never once ratted on me.

CHAPTER II

We lived on South Baker Street which was in a good neighborhood. From the front, our white frame house looked like it had two stories, but this was misleading because the only room upstairs was my brother Billy's bedroom. Downstairs were two more bedrooms, one for Dad and Mom and one for me. Also downstairs was a living room, a kitchen, a small dining room, and a bathroom. Dad had bought the house with a V.A. loan when he came home from Korea and went to work for the railroad. The place was run down, and had been vacant for several years, but Dad fixed it up so it looked pretty nice.

We were the only railroaders on South Baker Street. Most of the other homes were owned by doctors, lawyers, or college professors. Some people said we didn't belong in the neighborhood, but Dad said, "if a man works to get some place, then he belongs there."

Four blocks up the street was Idaho State University.

Dad said the university housed the greatest collection of nitwits in the world. He said they should put a fence around the place to keep the Communist lunatics from escaping. Dad called anyone he didn't like a Communist.

Dad was sitting on the front step waiting for us when we got home. "What happened to you?" he looked at my black eye.

"I ran into a limb," I lied.

"Sure you did." Dad wasn't fooled. He'd been in plenty of fights in his time, so he knew when someone had been leaned on. He didn't say anything more; figured it had been a kid's fight and something he'd better stay out of.

My Dad was a short stocky guy, five feet five inches. The top of his thinning head came to my chin. He was Irish so his face was mostly round and only what hair he had left wasn't red, but brown like his eyes. My Dad used to laugh a lot and that was all right. But sometimes he used to laugh at himself, like after he'd been hurt or someone had bested him in a deal. I thought that was kooky. When I got hurt, I started throwing things.

Dad was forty-five and worked in the Steel Car shop of the Union Pacific Railroad. His job was to fix beat-up freight cars. "The Irish built the Union Pacific and I'm going to keep it going," he said.

Dad went to work a half hour early every day. "I owe them that much because they gave me a job when nobody else would," he said. I thought that was stupid.

"All right, let's go," said Dad. "No slouching."

Dad worked all the time, fixing this, mending that. He thought everyone else should do the same, especially me. Only I didn't feel that way. Let things wait, that was my motto. Dad called it "slouching."

"Uncle Al going?" I asked.

"No," said Dad.

Uncle Al was Dad's brother. Sometimes he helped us with the ranch chores.

"Where'd Billy go?" asked Dad.

"He's around back getting water for that worthless mutt, Duke," I said.

We'd had another Black Lab before Duke. That dog's name had been Porky. And he was a real dog. Once he leaped after a wounded duck from a ten foot bank. Never seen a dog more water crazy than Porky.

My Dad shot Porky; shot him on purpose. I thought I'd never forgive him for that. Shortly after Porky was murdered, Dad got that Duke dog. Only Duke wasn't half the dog Porky was.

Billy came around the house smiling. Probably because it was Saturday and he didn't have to go to school. Billy didn't do well at his studies. He mostly got C's and once in a while a B. But it wasn't because he didn't study, because every night he brought work home, and him and Mom would work at the kitchen table. Still Billy didn't do well.

"I'll tell you what's your problem," I told him once. "You're stupid. Just plain stupid!" I talked to him like that because I knew Mom wasn't around. And because I'd never gotten a B in my life. Not one! All A's for every year I'd gone to school and I was sixteen and a sophomore in high school and Billy was 12, and in the seventh grade.

When I said that to Billy, I thought he'd cry, but he didn't. "I'll try harder," he said. "I'll show you." And he kept studying until Mom made him quit and go to bed.

We piled into Dad's old Chevy pickup; not real old, a '68. Dad gripped the steering wheel harder than he needed to. It was a habit. Sometimes on rutty roads the wheel would be jerked out of his hands. "Gonna break my wrist someday," laughed Dad. So even on the city streets he held the wheel tighter than need be.

We drove up South Baker Street then turned onto Railroad Avenue which took us over the tracks. Dad always slowed when we went over the tracks, so he could see how many "Red-tagged cars" were in the yard. Red-tagged cars were ones that needed work and would be pushed into the Steel Car Shop for repairs.

After we crossed the tracks, we drove parallel with them for about ten minutes, then turned up Jimmy Creek. Our ranch was two miles up the creek, at the end of the road.

It's a big place, over one and a half sections, almost a thousand acres. Some said that railroad people had no business owning a ranch like that, and maybe they're right. But when the place came up for sale nobody else much wanted it. "No water," the real estate people had said. "A creek that may or may not run all year, hills, and rocks. That's the Judge's place." What they said was mostly true, and that's why it sold cheap.

About that time Mom got an inheritance from an uncle back East, so she and Dad took the money and bought the Judge's old place. So that's how we came to own the ranch. A couple of years ago, a manufacturing plant came to Pocatello and after that more businesses. Property values sky-rocketed and the real estate people began to think that maybe the Judge's old place wasn't so dry and rocky as they figured and they came around offering the folks a lot of money for the ranch. But that didn't cut any ice because my Dad had worked hard on the place and he and Mom wouldn't sell it for any amount of money.

The first year we had the ranch, Dad planted wheat. Dad worked hard on that crop. Right after work at the railroad he went up to do the plowing, then after that the planting and the spraying. He worked late every night and on Saturday and Sunday too.

The crop came up looking pretty good and it seemed for awhile like we'd make some money. Then toward the end of June, the wheat turned black. "Smut," said Dad.

Smut's a fungus that attacks cereal grains. There are different kinds of smut but the kind we had infects the wheat heads, eating away the kernels until all that is left is a black ball of foul smelling powder.

We had smut all over the place. The wheat wasn't even worth cutting. When we found out what had happened, I thought Dad would sit down and cry. But he didn't. He shook his head a couple of times and laughed at himself, then got out the plow and turned her all under and planted pasture.

Dad loved that place more than anything in the world. Sometimes he would pick up a handful of soil, sniff it, then kiss it. Once when it rained, I saw him lay in the dirt face up and let the rain strike him just like it did the ground. I thought those were real dumb things to do, but I didn't say anything.

Near where we turned onto Jimmy Creek to go up to the ranch, buildings from an old hatchery sat rotting in a field at the mouth of the road. Old lady Smith had had a good business, lots of chickens, eggs, and customers. But then rich people thought it would be nice to build a house amidst the Juniper trees on Jimmy Creek. Shortly after that, men from the county office found lots of things wrong with Mrs. Smith's hatchery and they closed her down.

"Could happen to us some day," muttered Dad every time we passed the place. "A little guy has something the fat cats want and they'll badger you until they get it." He gripped the wheel of the Chevy harder.

After the hatchery, the road wound up around the hill. Lots of big new houses on each side. Rich people lived there. "People with more money than sense," my Uncle Al always said. "Look at them Juniper trees right up against the houses. Those trees are going to burn, it's just a matter of time. Some kid smoking will throw down a match, and the fire will creep through the June grass, then catch the branches of those trees. For a minute they'll flare, then "bang" they'll explode. It's happened before and it'll happen again."

That day the houses were still there and the junipers hadn't burned.

The ranch was at the top of a little hill. On the way up, on each side of the road was a large field of about forty acres. The West field had never been cultivated. It was overgrown with sagebrush and wild rose. At one time the East field had grown winter wheat, but for the last few years had been let go to weeds. Past these fields was the gate to our ranch.

The sheriff's car and an ambulance were parked on the road. The sheriff and the county coroner were in the weed field studying something on a stretcher. "Now what?" Dad said. He parked in front of our gate and we got out to see what was going on.

The coroner's name was Steve Amond. He was a short fat guy with a round, red face because he drank too much. Besides being the county coroner he also worked at the hospital, helping the pathologist with autopsies.

He'd been coroner for ten years, because the only one that ever ran against him was Curt Dunning, the mortician. No one liked either one of them, but they disliked Amond less than Dunning, so Amond got elected.

The sheriff's name was Abe Solomon. He was a Jew. Most towns have Hebe bankers or tailors, but Pocatello had a Jewish sheriff. That was sort of funny. Abe Solomon was a big skinny guy, about six two. Like me, he had red hair. Jews aren't supposed to have red hair, but Abe Solomon did, so I suppose there's Jewish guys like that.

Abe wore his sheriff's uniform; he always did; was proud of it, and kept it looking real sharp. Steve Amond was wearing those green pajama-like things you see in doctor movies. He got them free from the hospital.

As we walked across the field the sheriff raised his hand in greeting. "Hello Abe," said Dad. He nodded his head in respect. "Hello Steve."

I stopped several yards from the two men. The smell from the figure on the stretcher nauseated me. I thought I'd get sick. Billy and Dad kept going. "Got a stiff here, Frank," said the sheriff. "You know him?"

The corpse was dressed in cowboy boots, Levi pants and shirt, most of the buttons were popped off the shirt due to bloating. Dad studied the corpse several minutes. "Nope," he finally said. "I don't believe I know him. Big guy, and dark. Looks like an Indian."

"That's what we think," said the coroner. He picked up a stick and scraped maggots away from the stiff's nose and mouth.

"How long you figure he's been here?" asked Dad.

"I won't know for sure till the Doc does the autopsy," said the coroner. "From the looks of him, I'd say at least four days."

22

"Funny we never saw him," said Dad. "We come by here two or three times a day. Who found him?"

"A kid walking his dog," said the sheriff. "You got any Indians working for you on the place, Frank?"

"Nope," said Dad. He grinned. "I can hardly afford to pay my boys here. You recognize this man, Billy?"

"No!" Billy had been staring at the body. He shook his head.

I'd gotten over my squeamishness and stood near the corpse.

"How about you, Davy?" asked Dad. "You know this guy?"

"No," I said. "Not with him being all puffed up and stinking. But he looks familiar, like someone I know. Might be related to Andy Echo." Andy was my friend at Pocatello High School.

"Why sure! Bright boy!" The sheriff grinned and tossled my hair. "It's Willie Echo. Should have seen it right away, had him in the slammer often enough."

"How you suppose he got here?" I asked. "Been shot?"

"No!" Steve Amond laughed. "No marks that I can see. Whiskey bottles on the ground up by your gate. He was probably up here at night drinking with his friends, got boozed up, and ran off. Then lay in the weeds and died. Happens a lot."

"A waste!" Dad took me and Billy by the shoulder and steered us back to the car. "Big young guy like that drinking himself to death."

I unlocked the gate and we drove the quarter mile down to the ranch house. Dad looked at our fields. They were greening up good.

Below the house was the corral where we kept Tiberius, our hereford bull. Tiberius lay in a corner of the corral and lazily watched us drive up. It was April. We were still feeding hay to our twenty-five cow herd. In another month Tiberius would be turned in with the herd where he would earn his keep as a cowpuncher.

Tiberius was a ton of the meanest bull that ever lived. Dad had bought him at a dispersal sale. A rancher smarter than us had decided to call it quits and was selling his whole herd. Dad paid twenty-five hundred dollars for that bull. Mom had a fit, but Dad insisted it was a necessary investment if we ever hoped to improve our breeding.

Well I felt the money was a total waste. Every time I came near him that bull rolled his eyes, shook his head and got to snorting. With Billy it was different. He walked right up to Tiberius, rubbed his ears and scratched his back, and the bull just stood there liking every minute of it.

The ranch house, more of a cabin than a house, had a large living room with a big stone fireplace, then a small kitchen and bathroom. Above the kitchen was a loft that served as a bedroom. Judge Burch who'd bought the several pieces and put the ranch together in the 30's and 40's, had the cabin built in 1948. In the evenings he played poker with the boys. At night he played with the girls. His mark was everywhere at the ranch. O.R.B. for Oliver Robert Burch burned into the wall near the sink in the kitchen. O. R. Burch on the nameplate on the door. O.R.B. + J.D. L. for Janet Doris Larsen, his most steady girlfriend, scratched into the arm rest on the chair.

I'll tell you about the Judge.

He'd been district judge for one term when it came to the public's attention that the judge's money and the county's was getting mixed up, with most of it going into the Judge's pocket. Reluctantly, by a landslide, the voters threw him out of office. Still, ever after, he kept the title of Judge Burch.

The Judge had been dead five years, but lived on in the cabin. No one else knew he was there, but I could feel his spirit, and hear him arguing with himself before the fireplace. If I closed my eyes, I could see the time him and a new girlfriend, Elaine, were sitting on the couch. Could see Janet Doris, her long blond hair streaming down her back, her blue eyes on fire with jealousy enter with a shotgun and point it at the Judge. I could see Elaine shield the judge with her body and say, "Go ahead. If that's what you want Janet, shoot."

And Janet threw down the gun and left weeping. Only

later it was Janet Doris and the Judge who went back together.

If I closed my eyes real tight, I could see the Judge lying naked on the floor. He'd fallen down in the middle of one of his wild parties. Worried guests had called a doctor.

The doctor found his way up to the cabin. He was new, a cocky young man who didn't know the Judge. Anyway, the Judge lay on the floor naked and the doctor stood over him. "Who are you?" the Judge opened one eye and looked up.

"I'm the devil come for your soul." The doctor thought himself clever.

"Shiiit!" said the Judge and he rolled over and died.

Janet Doris disappeared after the funeral. No one knew where she went. I had a hunch that one day she'd return to the cabin to be with the Judge.

The young doctor also left a few months after the funeral. No one engaged his services. He was too clever for the people of Pocatello.

When he'd been alive, I'd known the Judge. Like most everyone I'd been charmed by his smile and warm familiarity. Unlike many, I'd been lucky. I was a small boy and didn't have any money to be conned out of. So in life I'd held no hard feelings against the Judge, and now in death, I guess he held me none. I saw him often, felt his presence more, and sensed that he tolerated me in his cabin.

Behind the cabin, its banks bordered by birch and hawthorne trees, flowed Jimmy Creek. On the other side of the creek rose a hill. There were a few pine trees at the base of the hill but farther up grew only cedar trees and sagebrush. Near the top was an Indian burial ground. Maybe a dozen graves in all.

Before we got the ranch, people went up there and dug around for beads and artifacts. But no more. "Leave them be," Dad said. "They had little enough when alive. No sense bothering them now."

Well, that day we dropped Billy off to take care of Tiberius, while Dad and I went up to where the cattle lazed in winter pasture.

We had a stack of baled hay with a board fence around it. "We've only got another month to feed," said Dad. "So give each cow a half bale." That was pretty good for the cows, more than thirty pounds; most guys only fed fifteen or twenty.

"No new calves." Dad looked the herd over carefully. We ear tagged any new calf the day it was born. That way we didn't mix up the mothers. We were about done calving. Only five left to go.

Dad and I pitched the hay over the fence to the cows. We threw over as many bales as needed, then took the twine off and scattered the hay around so a few old boss cows wouldn't get it all.

We weren't half done and sweat rolled down my forehead into my eyes. Dad wasn't even perspiring.

"You've got to get some rhythm into you," he told me. "Muscles are one thing, but no good without rhythm. Otherwise you tire too easily."

"So what," I thought. "There's more to life than pitching hay."

I could see the roof of Zane Bodkins' shack. No smoke came from the chimney. Zane was in town drinking.

We weren't done but I climbed the fence and went toward the cabin.

"Where are you going?" asked Dad.

"To the bathroom," I lied. I was tired. Dad could finish. After he was done he'd go fool around with the new corral he was building, then he'd stop and put a few rocks on Porky's cairn.

He shot Porky in the winter. It was too cold to dig a grave so he'd built a cairn out in the pasture. That was something—shoot a dog then make a fool of yourself by every day adding to his cairn.

The cairn wasn't the only stupid thing my Dad did. In the upper field was an old orchard put in by the guy that had homesteaded the place. The trees did well because of a gully with a little spring that had plenty of water.

One fall Dad and I were up there looking around, and we came upon an old stallion. When the Judge died there were about fifty horses roaming the place. It had taken a long time to get somebody to round them up and take them away. The stallion had hid out up in that draw.

The thing could hardly walk but he was plenty mean, pulling his lips back like he wanted to bite, and putting his rump toward you so that you knew he'd kick your head off.

"I'll shoot him," I said. I had my Savage with me.

"Let him be, son," said Dad. My Dad didn't act like a guy that had served in the front lines of Korea. He hardly ever wanted to kill anything.

Next spring we went up that gulch. All that was left of the stallion was a pile of bones and a few pieces of hide that the magpies hadn't bothered about. I was plenty glad about it, but Dad acted sort of strange. He grabbed my arm. "Son I want you to promise me something," he said. Not waiting for me to say yes or no, he went on. "Promise me that when I die you'll bury me up in this draw."

Boy, now I thought that was stupid. What with modern medicine, people just didn't die any more only in the newspaper. "All right. I promise Dad." I said it quick like, cause he was hurting my arm. Still Dad didn't let go for a long time, like he'd suddenly seen something and was afraid.

After that we went down and I never went up that draw until after Dad was shot.

In front of the cabin was a gravel parking place and then there were two piles of log fence posts about three feet tall. I was supposed to move the posts, but hadn't gotten around to it. I went into the cabin. The judge sat before the fireplace with a drink in his hand. As usual, he was naked. "They found a dead Indian outside the gate." I told him. The Judge didn't look up, just crinkled his nose. He knew all about it.

The Judge put his drink down and acted like he was going to say something, then changed his mind and went back to his booze.

Dad and Billy came in. They didn't see the Judge. Billy picked up my Model 99 Savage that stood in the corner.

"When you going to clean this?" He acted like he knew all about guns.

"When I'm good and ready!" I said.

"You better be ready now," said Dad. It made him mad when someone neglected a weapon. He had a Browning 30-06 semi-automatic rifle that he always kept in top shape. My Uncle Al had a Remington 7 mm bolt action rifle. Uncle Al said the gun wasn't any good because it kept jamming, but it wasn't the gun's fault. Uncle Al reloaded his own shells and he never sized them properly so he had to dig about every fourth one out of the chamber. But you couldn't tell Uncle Al that. Nobody could tell Uncle Al anything, except maybe my Dad.

"I'll take it home today and clean it." I took the Savage from Billy.

"See that you do," said Dad. Billy grinned. He'd scored a point. I felt like smashing him.

We went out and locked the doors, then drove down to the gate. The sheriff and coroner were gone, but a new fella was out in the field where they found Willie Echo.

"Who is he?" Billy whispered. The guy was skinny and tall. He wore a wrinkled blue suit, white shirt, but no tie. He had a camera around his neck.

"A reporter," I said. "Probably from the *News*." The guy shot a picture of Billy and me, then he came up. Dad stayed in the truck and watched through the rear view mirror.

"Howdy boys." The guy tried to act friendly. Only I didn't think he meant it. I looked in his eyes. They were brown and shifty.

"Who are you?" I wasn't nice. Billy winced. He liked to be friends with everyone.

"My name is Phil Snuder." The reporter held out his hand. I didn't want to take it, but did. "I'm an investigative reporter for the *Pocatello News*."

So what, I thought. The guy had a way of looking that made me uneasy. Like the way guys look at you in the men's room at the bus station. His hair looked like those guys too; bald up front then stringy in back down to his collar. Goofy looking that's what I called it.

I could take him, I knew that. Maybe three punches, that's all it would take.

"That's a nice camera you have." Billy went to touch Phil Snuder's camera. The reported jumped back.

"Yes, it is, but don't touch it, little boy," he said.

"Why not?" asked Billy.

"Cause it's a Hasselblad," said the reporter. "Cost over four thousand dollars."

"Wow," said Billy. "Why so much?"

"Cause it's good," said Snuder. "It was with a Hasselblad that Neil Armstrong took the first pictures of earth from his space ship *The Eagle.*"

"Now there's a bunch of crap," I said. "The fact is the picture was taken by Frank Borman from *Apollo 8.*" Snuder didn't like that, but I didn't care. "Come on Billy," I said. "Dad's getting impatient." I snapped the lock on the gate.

"One more picture, boys?" Snuder didn't wait to see if we agreed, just started snapping pictures.

Billy winced. He didn't like people taking his picture. Never had. Used to hide during the family pictures, Dad had to pull him out from under the couch.

We pushed by the reporter and got into the pickup. "Who is that guy?" asked Dad.

"A reporter," Billy said.

"What is he up to?" Dad wrinkled his forehead. He shouldn't do that; too many lines already.

"Sniffing around about the Indian," I said.

"Communists," said Dad. Like I said, Dad called anyone he didn't like a Communist. He gripped the wheel and tried to dodge the chuckholes in the road. He wasn't entirely successful. We drove on home.

CHAPTER III

Uncle Al banged the door Sunday morning. I let him in and poured a cup of coffee from the pot Mom had put on the timer. Uncle Al took the cup and warmed his hands along the outside. "Cream or sugar?" I knew he didn't want either, but asked so I'd hear his answer.

"Nope! Take my coffee like my women; strong, black, and hot." He laughed at his joke. He wasn't married so he could talk like that. Dad seldom made those kind of jokes. If he did Mom would look at him funny and start asking a lot of questions.

Uncle Al had been a soldier for fifteen years. He'd been a Green Beret, fought in Vietnam, and came back a captain. Not the biggest guy in the world, five eight, only heavy and mean tough. He was always punching or wrestling around. Even at work, he got to punching.

A guy like Uncle Al can get into a lot of trouble, and most places wouldn't keep him on. Only he worked hard, and showed up sober, and since he'd about run out of "tough guys" to punch, Paul De Gamma, the foreman at the steel car shop, overlooked a lot of things.

Uncle Al would still be in the army, only after the Vietnam War they had a cut-back; bounced all the reserve officers and only kept Regular Army. That's what Uncle Al said, but Dad told Mom different.

"When its war, they need guys like Al . . . gutty guys to lead the charge, blow the bridges, and like that picture in *Newsweek* of Al, dragging a wounded buddy back to the line. That's the kind they need when the going is tough, but not later. In peacetime you can't have guys like that around with all their medals, when what is needed is sweet talk and booze and parties at the Officers' Club and favors for the politicians. Then guys like Al can be an embarrassment. They might even hurt someone. Find an excuse to get rid of them. That's what my Dad said about Uncle Al and the army.

"Looks like you made the paper." Uncle Al had brought the Sunday *News* with him.

"What about?" Billy was still in his pajamas but had heard us talking and came down.

"About that dead Indian on your place," Uncle Al said.

"He wasn't on our place," I said. "They found him in the field below the gate."

"Not according to Phil Snuder."

"Who is Phil Snooper?" asked Billy. He didn't have a good memory.

"Not Snooper, Snuder," laughed Uncle Al. "He's the latest import, here to enlighten us hayseeds as to the real meaning of the news."

"Must have been that weasel looking guy who was taking my picture," said Billy.

"He's made you famous," said Uncle Al. "Got a picture of you and Davy closing the gate. Makes it look like the field where the Indian died is on the inside."

"What's this Snooper fellow got to say?" I asked.

"Plenty!" Uncle Al laughed. Thought it funny the way

we misused the reporter's name. "Distinguished Native American found dead in the vicinity of McGrath ranch."

About then Dad and Mom came in. Dad was wearing only pants and a tee shirt. Mom was dressed for church. Uncle Al showed them the article in the news. Dad went out on the porch to get our paper. Billy tried to get at the comics, but Dad wouldn't let him. Uncle Al gave Billy the comics out of his *News*. Uncle Al would give Billy anything he wanted.

"Distinguished Native American found dead in vicinity of McGrath Ranch," Dad read. "Willie Echo is thought to have been examining ancient Shoshone burial ground when he died under mysterious circumstances."

"Oh crap!" said Mom. She looked at Billy and me and blushed. Mom didn't often use such language. Billy and I laughed. We had one on her.

"Then it goes on to say," read Dad. "Willie Echo was born on the Wind River Reservation in Wyoming and moved to Fort Hall as a child where he enjoyed hunting and fishing."

"Why don't they also say that he liked to chase women and drink himself into a stupor?" said Mom.

"They're saving that obituary for me," said Uncle Al.

Mom looked at him and frowned.

"In the end," read Pa. "It says that the U.S. Marshall's Office is investigating the death of Willie Echo, and also the matter of the desecration of the Indian burial ground."

"What's to investigate?" said Uncle Al. "There isn't a dozen graves on that hill and no one has been up there since you got the place. Besides, before us White Eyes came, the Skins stuffed their dead in the fork of a tree and rode off."

"There's an old white graveyard up on City Creek," said Mom. "Houses are built on it now. And there was an Indian graveyard on Fifteenth where they built apartments. Why don't they investigate them?"

My Mom was a little, round woman; round red head, round face, round body; everything round. But she wasn't fat and men found her attractive. Didn't seem right that she had a string bean son like me.

"I'll get to the bottom of this," said Dad. He went to the kitchen phone and called Abe Solomon.

"Hello Abe," Dad said. "This is Frank McGrath. Sorry to bother you on Sunday, but I been reading the article in the *News* about that dead Indian and wondered what you found out about it."

"Nothing much to it," said the sheriff. "The guy had been drinking at Nick's Place. When the bar closed, he and some buddies took a bottle and drove up your road to finish it off. The stuff finally got to Willie Echo. He started yelling, then ran into the field. His buddies were too drunk to worry about him and after they'd finished the bottle, drove into town. Nobody gave Willie any thought until that kid found him yesterday. Guess he laid down in the field and died. 'Death from acute alcoholic intoxication,' the pathologist said."

"That's all?" asked Dad.

"That's it," said Abe Solomon.

"Then what's all this stuff about mysterious death, and Sacred Indian Burial Ground?"

The sheriff laughed. "That's investigative reporting," he said. "If there's no news, then you make some. New reporter! Got to make a name for himself. I hope he doesn't stir things up too much. Don't worry about it, Frank."

"I'll try not to," said Dad. "Thanks Abe."

Mom brought the coffee pot in and filled Uncle Al's cup then poured some for Dad and her. I pushed a cup toward the pot, but she ignored me. "Are we going to lose the ranch, Frank?" she asked.

That idea really bothered Dad. "Hell no!" he said. "How could we? The Indians sold the land at the turn of the century. People homesteaded it, then the Judge bought it."

"Still, I don't like it," said Mom. "Things have a way of getting twisted. Those people always seem to get what they want."

"Yeah," said Uncle Al. "And when they do, there's somebody from the government there to see that nobody interferes."

Dad looked at Uncle Al sour like. It was all right for him to criticize the government, but he didn't like anybody else doing the same.

"We're making too much of this." Dad got up and started rummaging in the cupboard. "Let's do like Abe Solomon says and forget it."

Mom took the hint from Dad's rummaging and started fixing breakfast. "You staying, Al?" she asked.

"Might as well," said Uncle Al. "My girlfriend likes to sleep late on Sunday and probably doesn't have anything ready." Mom shot him a mean look, but didn't say anything.

The grownups acted like they were going to forget about the news article, but I wasn't. Tomorrow at school I'd ask Andy Echo what was going on.

CHAPTER IV

I'll tell you about Andy Echo. Andy Echo lived at Fort Hall or more precisely he lived up Ross Fork Creek, about seven miles from the tribal headquarters and town called Fort Hall. Andy is my size, only with a better build. By that I mean he's fatter. But I can take him; not that we'd ever had a fight because we hadn't. Yet lots of time we wrestled around and its from that, I knew if I had to, I could take him.

Andy's Dad was on the Fort Hall business council, which was a good job. Andy once told me that his father made over a thousand dollars a month. Also he got his house free, the tribe paid his utilities, and he could charge his groceries to the tribe. All in all it seemed like a good deal.

The Ross Fork Valley is broad and grassy. On each side are sage covered hills and in the distance looms Mount

37

Putnam. Andy was lucky to live there but I still wouldn't trade our ranch on Jimmy Creek.

Once Andy had me out to help him with a quarter-horse colt. The colt was a little skittish, but not mean, and we had him broke to lead in a short time.

After we were through with the colt, Andy's mother had us in for cocoa and cookies. Their house was real nice. Andy told me it had three bathrooms and two fireplaces. How they could use more than one bathroom or fireplace at a time was a mystery to me, but I didn't say anything. It has to do with conspicuous consumption like Mr. Ravelli taught in economics class.

Andy's mother was a big, pleasant woman. I'd heard that her husband got drunk and batted her around. But she looked all right to me, so I didn't know if that story was true or not.

That day was the first time I saw Andy's Dad, Harry Echo. He was six feet and maybe two hundred and fifty pounds. He had a big, bushy head of black Indian hair and one of those jaws that stick out at you. I didn't think I could take him.

Harry Echo walked kind of stiff. Andy said that was because he had a hernia and all the time had to wear a truss. Mr. Echo had a funny way of talking. He never looked you in the face. I couldn't understand that mannerism. I'd been taught not to trust a man who wouldn't look you in the eye, and that sure turned out to be true in this case. I'll have more to say about that later.

Sometimes Andy Echo and I spent hours talking about things no one else believed but we knew to be true. I told him about the ghost of the Judge up at the ranch, and sometimes seeing the old stallion that had died grazing out in the field.

Andy believed me but when I'd had him up to the ranch, he couldn't see the Judge even though the old barrister had stood naked as a jaybird in front of him. Andy hadn't been able to catch sight of the horse either, but then I guess those things were reserved for me.

"I'll tell you about the Water Babies," Andy said. "They

are called Pahonahs. The Shoshones used to believe that it was bad medicine to have twins. When this happened the mother choked one and threw it in the creek."

"People aren't supposed to believe this anymore, but some women still do. Have you ever seen a pair of Indian twins?" I hadn't.

"There's more about those water babies, too," he said. "After they are thrown into the water, they don't die, but turn into demons. During the day they hide in bushes along the bank. At night they come out, splash around, and set up a plaintive wail. They try to lure people near so they can drag them into the water and suck their blood.

"There was an old man whose name was George," said Andy. "This George guy got lost on the reservation at night, and the next day when they found him he was sucked dry by the water babies."

So, like I said, Andy Echo and I had been pretty good friends and I saw him at school the day after the article came out in the *News* about his Uncle Willie.

The buses unloaded behind the high school on Garfield Avenue. Andy Echo usually came in on the bus from Tyhee, the town nearest the reservation. He got to Tyhee on a special bus from Fort Hall. When he missed the Tyhee bus, then the reservation bus brought him all the way in. Not many Indian kids went to high school, and those that did got to go to the school of their choice. Andy was the only Indian kid at Pocatello High, we called it Poky High.

When I got to school, I went around to the bus stop to find Andy. His back was to me, but I spotted him easy. He always wore blue Levis and a white shirt; blue and white, the favorite Indian colors.

"Hi Andy!" I put my hand on his shoulder

He jerked away. His face was mean looking and he acted like he wanted to hit me, only didn't. "You white son-of-a-bitch," he said.

"Why are you talking like that?"

"You killed my Uncle Willie," he said.

"You're crazy! Willie drank himself to death. You know it!" And Andy did know it. I could tell by his eyes. They lost that black mean look and got sort of glassy. He was lying and his eyes showed it.

"You killed him," repeated Andy. "And my Dad's going to get you!" He hit me in the mouth, then turned and ran up the stairs to school.

I could have caught him, but didn't. Fact is I was too shocked to think. I'd never before been hit by a friend. Besides it didn't hurt.

The guys that had stood watching us, hoping for a fight, turned and followed Andy. I licked the blood from my lips and stood trying to think. The bell rang, and I took the stairs two at a time.

So his dad's going to get me, I thought. Wonder what that means? I tried not to let the threat bother me, but it did. I missed two on the Spanish test. I usually didn't miss any. "I won't worry about it anymore," I promised myself. "I can't take Harry Echo, but I think Dad can and Uncle Al sure as hell can! That should settle it."

"I see you got some bad press," Mr. Ravelli told me in science class. Mr. Ravelli was a short, stocky Italian; black hair, white teeth, swarthy skin, the works. He wore bright vests and checkered pants; pretty loud clothes for Pocatello, but I thought it was neat.

I was lots taller than Mr. Ravelli, but I didn't think I could take him. Got to watch out for short Wops. They can be tricky. Mr. Ravelli and I got along good.

"Yeah," I said. "Some real bad press."

"What you going to do about it?" he asked.

"I don't know," I said. "Hard to fight a headline."

"You're right kid," said Mr. Ravelli. "Damned hard." When we were alone Mr. Ravelli sometimes used strong language. "So don't try to fight them. Outlast them. In time they dry up and blow away."

"You serious?" I asked. "Do nothing?"

"That's right kid," he said. "Do nothing."

After school, I walked home with Steely Marks. Steely was not his real name. His real name was Gregory, but when he was eight years old he got caught taking a package of lifesavers from the drugstore, so kids got to calling him

Steely. Only most people didn't know that's how he got his name. They thought it was because of his mouse colored hair.

Steely's hair went to his shoulders. That was cool. My Dad made me wear my hair short. When I got older, I'd tell Dad to go jump and wear my hair any way I wanted.

I could take Steely.

He was a big kid, even taller than me. But he was real skinny and had pimples. I thought that was because he smoked.

"You want a cigarette?" said Steely. He smoked Lucky Strikes, those without filters. No pimp sticks for Steely, real coffin nails.

"No," I said for the thousandth time. I had planned to go to college, had a good chance too with my grades and my running. I was the best high school miler in the state. Could run it in four minutes, twenty seconds, which wasn't bad. Already some college coaches had been around to talk to me.

I didn't want a cigarette hack lousing everything up. "You ought to quit," I said to Steely. "You're getting skinnier and skinnier."

"Don't want to," said Steely. He didn't look at me, and I knew it had gone beyond the point of wanting to. Fact is, old Steely was hooked on the weed.

"See by the paper you had to kill an Indian," said Steely.

"I didn't kill anyone. He drank himself to death."

"Sure," said Steely. But I knew he didn't believe me. The *News* implied that Willie was murdered and that was good enough for Steely.

We walked without saying anything more. Steely cupped his cigarette in his hands so no one would know he was smoking, but of course everyone did.

A block from his house Steely threw his cigarette in the gutter, then took several deep breaths to clear his lungs. His folks were big in the Mormon Church, and would have a fit if they knew Steely smoked.

"See you tomorrow," said Steely when we got to his house.

"Not tomorrow," I said. "It's an In Day." An In Day stands for In Service when there's no school because the teachers are supposed to do some work.

"That's right," said Steely. He was going to go into the house, then stopped. "Watch out Davy," he said. "Andy Echo is saying that his Dad's going to get you."

"I know," I said. "Thanks!" I turned toward home.

CHAPTER V

Mom was looking out the door for the paper. The *Pocatello News* came out every afternoon but Saturday. Dad said that "by Saturday all the newspaper people were too drunk to get a paper out."

Sometimes the paper didn't even come out during the week. When we called up, a girl said: "The presses broke down."

"Hah," said Dad. "Those Communists are all drunk again."

Dad was almost as hard on drinking as he was the Communists. That was because he used to drink a lot himself, and one night got thrown in the drunk tank at the police station.

Of course that was before, when a drunk was just a drunk, and not some poor soul with a disease. "I'd rather be a drunk than diseased," said Dad.

Anyway one night in the drunk tank sobered him up

and he never took another drink, and he was mad at anyone who did, even Uncle Al, who had sense enough not to come around when he had a few beers, which was quite often.

Mom went back in the house. I sat on the steps and waited. The *News* hadn't come yet. After awhile I saw the kid coming with the paper.

Our paper boy's name is Wayne Briggs. He rides a yellow ten speed bicycle. Usually he throws our paper in the shrubs beside the porch, but when he saw me he decided to come up the walk and hand it to me. "You're smart," I said to him.

"How's that?" He asked.

"Cause if you'd thrown the paper in the bushes I'd have wrapped that ten speed around your scrawny neck." Wayne Briggs swallowed hard, and continued down the block.

We didn't make page one where all the national and international news was printed, but we were on page two. A small article in the corner under the obituaries stated: "The mysterious death of Willie Echo on Jimmy Creek was still being investigated."

Dad drove in the driveway then; his face was black like it always was at the end of work. He took the paper away from me. When he came home, the paper was his and there was no argument about it. He sat next to me on the porch. I moved over; didn't want his dirty pants brushing me.

The article about the continued investigation didn't impress him. He grunted. Higher on the page was a picture and an article about NOI, the National Organization for Indians. Russell Jones, the president of NOI, had been invited to speak the next day at the University. "Communists!" said Dad.

"Who?" I was reading over his shoulder. "Russell Jones or the University?"

"Both," said Dad. He rattled the paper. "Particularly the University. They pay out taxpayers money to invite any queer and Communist in the country to come and speak."

"It's students' funds," I said. We'd argued that before. Like I said, Dad felt they should build a fence around Idaho State University so that none of the kooky professors could escape.

During the Vietnam War people from the university used to have "Peace marches" on South Baker Street. One time Dad stepped out on the porch and beaned a marcher with a soy sauce bottle. Knocked him down and out. The other marchers helped the victim to his feet then went down town to the old post office where they pulled down the American Flag.

Later a policeman came to our house with a complaint that Dad had thrown the soy sauce bottle. "I don't know anything about anything," said Dad.

"Okay," the policeman smiled. He was a war vet. "That's good enough for me." He went away.

"What do you mean, student funds?" Dad turned on me. "It's parents' money, that's what it is!" I didn't argue anymore. Those speeches were a real sore spot with Dad.

Russell Jones looked like an Indian; that said something for him. Most of the guys in NOI looked more white than Indian, but not Jones. He wore his black hair in long braids that hung on each side of his skinny face. He had a humped, nickel nose, and a thin mean mouth that never smiled. He was a tall guy, but you couldn't tell that by the photo.

In addition to Russell Jones, the picture also showed Loretta Cager, and Harry Echo. You know who Harry Echo was, but I'll tell you about Loretta Cager.

Loretta was on the Fort Hall Business Council. She had been born out there, then went to Haskell Institute at Lawrence, Kansas. Haskell was a government boarding school for Indians.

When she was at Haskell, she got hooked up with Russell Jones. Andy Echo told me she and Russell may even have gotten married, but no one knows for sure. What was known was that she had two children by someone, then came home and dumped the kids on her mother, and ran off to join the Indian occupation of Alcatraz.

Apparently the occupation of Alcatraz Island didn't

work out the way it was planned, what with the government and everyone else willing to let the Indians sit it out as long as Al Capone or longer if they wanted.

One day Loretta Cager got up a collection to go to San Francisco to buy food. For all that is known the Indians on Alcatraz are still waiting for the food, because Loretta took off with the money, and the band's car and returned to Fort Hall.

For awhile she was pretty quiet, worried that maybe the people from NOI might come looking for her and their money. But after awhile when no one showed up, Loretta came out of hiding, got a government scholarship and said she was going to the University of Idaho at Moscow to become a lawyer and help her people.

Loretta was a pretty woman, thin, not fat like most Shoshone squaws and real light complected. Fact was she had to work hard to look like an Indian. She didn't last long at Moscow; was back in six months, and put her name up for the Fort Hall Business Council. "The run for the money," the people call it. Loretta was elected, and there she was in the paper between Russell Jones and Harry Echo.

While I was sitting on the steps trying to read over Dad's shoulder, Mom came out. "Better come in and change out of your school clothes, Davy," she said. I went in and put on a pair of brown levis and a green plaid shirt, then hung up my school clothes. This was pretty good for me because I usually didn't hang things up.

By the time I was finished changing it was time to eat. I waved at Wee Willie, then left my room. Wee Willie was a garter snake I kept in an aquarium on my dresser. I'll tell you about him later.

Dad had washed up and was in the kitchen, and then Uncle Al came in. "You want to eat, Al?" asked Mom. He did, so we sat down.

Billy had been out back feeding Duke so was last to come in. Mom had cooked pork chops, mashed potatoes and gravy. Also okra in tomatoes, some people called it gumbo.

I ate two pork chops, and then when it looked like no one was going to eat what was left, I fished two more out of the pan. Uncle Al looked at me sort of mean like; he had been eyeing those two chops. I grinned and went on eating.

"You're not eating much," Mom said to Billy. He had only one chop, a few potatoes and hardly any gumbo.

"I'm saving myself for dessert." He'd been snooping in the kitchen and seen Mom's pies. Billy was a big dessert guy; would eat nothing but sweets if he had his choice.

"You eat more okra or you don't get any pie." Mom put another spoonful of okra in his bowl. Billy wrinkled his nose, but ate it.

For dessert we had strawberry pie. Billy got two helpings as was expected, then while I was still eating, Uncle Al managed to get the last piece of pie. He grinned at me; revenge for the pork chops.

"What did you think about that letter to the Editor?" Uncle Al asked Dad.

"I didn't see it," said Dad. He got the paper. The letter was the usual type written by an English professor at the University. The letter read:

> Dear Sir:
> The recent death of Willie Echo, a respected native American member of the community, is to be deplored. How long must the first Americans suffer the indignities of a foreign culture? Justice must return to this country, and the land returned to its rightful owners!
> Respectfully,
> Horace Butters, Ph.D.

"Crap!" said Dad. "Communist crap!"

"You might know an English teacher would write something like that," said Mom. She'd taken a semester of general studies at the university.

"Then why did the professor write the letter to the paper?" Billy asked.

"Because he's a Communist," said Dad. "The university is full of them. It bothers them when brave men stand and fight for what is right."

"Well, I don't know." Billy wasn't intimidated. He wrinkled his stub of a nose making the freckles fold on each other. "I'm going to look into this, then I'll let you know."

"You do that!" shouted Uncle Al. He leaned across the table until he was face to face with Billy. "By God you just do that!" More than anyone, Uncle Al liked Billy, yet they were always arguing.

"I will!" Billy laughed. "Later!"

Dad had taken the cribbage board and deck of cards that were always in the center of the table. He shuffled, then dealt Billy and himself a hand. Billy, still grinning at Uncle Al, set the pegs up in the board.

I would have rather gone up to the ranch and got the feeding over, but knew better than say anything. The nightly contest between Dad and Billy over the cribbage board took preference even over ranch work.

Uncle Al slurped his coffee while he watched the game. I pretended to read the paper. If I looked around, Mom might grab me to help with the dishes.

Dad won the game. "There!" He said. "That shows you." He beamed with satisfaction.

Billy laughed. He always did. He tried his best, and so win or lose, it was all the same. We piled into the pickup and went up to feed. Mom stayed with the dishes.

Billy and I got out to open the gate, then climbed into the back of the pickup for the quarter mile ride to the ranch house. I looked at the field where they had found Willie Echo. It was the same; couldn't even tell that two days before a man had been out there rotting in the sun.

Old Tiberius lay in his corral, and when he saw us he got up and started pawing the ground and swinging his bull head from side to side.

As soon as we stopped, Billy jumped over the tailgate, threw Tiberius some hay, then stood there scratching the big hereford's side. "Go right ahead," I said. "He's your bull, and you're welcome to him."

I walked up with Dad and Uncle Al to pitch hay to the cows. "No smoke from Zane Bodkins' chimney," said Dad. "He's probably in town hustling some squaw."

The cows were waiting near the stack. A few of the

calves looked up at us, then went back to sucking on their mothers. "Five more calves and it will be a hundred percent drop," I said. "Tiberius has done his job real good."

"In another month we'll turn him in to start over again," said Dad.

"Maybe then he won't be so snorty," I said. Uncle Al laughed.

It had been a mild winter and the stock looked good. We'd have a hold over of hay and that, too, was good. "Just like money in the bank," Dad said. "This year we'll have some extra to sell and with hay at fifty dollars a ton, that won't be hard to take, either."

We hadn't finished feeding, but I left and went down to the cabin. Dad shook his head when he saw me leave. "Slouching off again," he muttered.

I pretended not to hear. There wasn't much more to do and after that Dad and Uncle Al would go into the field to see if the grass they planted last fall was coming up. Then Dad would stop and put some rocks on Porky's cairn.

Billy was still fooling with Tiberius. I went into the cabin.

The judge had a fire going and was standing near the mantle to keep warm. Bottles were scattered everywhere. He'd been drinking heavy. "You'd be a lot warmer," I said. "If you put some clothes on."

The Judge looked at me and snorted. I figured he probably got that from Tiberius, although he didn't like that bull any more than I did. "How come you're so snorty?" I asked.

The Judge looked at me worried like. The bags under his eyes were heavier than usual. "What you need is Janet Doris," I said. "I'm going to find her and bring her up here."

I thought I was making a joke and hoped to see the Judge smile, but again he snorted and went to the window and pointed at Tiberius and Billy. "That old bull bothering you?" I said. "Don't worry nothing about him Judge. He's as much of a kid as Billy."

But the Judge did worry. Once he opened his mouth and I thought he'd say something but he didn't.

Dad and Uncle Al were in the pickup honking, so I left the house. It was cold, so on the way down, Billy and I crowded up front.

"What you going to do tomorrow?" Billy asked me.

"Go to the library and work on my science project," I replied. "Should be able to wrap it up. What you going to do?"

"Come up here and work with Tiberius," said Billy.

"Huh!" said Dad. "I'll tell you both where you're going. To school, that's where." Uncle Al grinned and nodded

Billy laughed. "No school tomorrow Pop. It's an In Day."

"Never had In Days when I went to school," said Dad. "The teachers got paid and they worked. Simple as that. Now they get paid and don't work."

"It's even simpler that way," said Uncle Al. He laughed at his joke. I didn't say anything. I was out of school. That was all that mattered. For Billy it would matter plenty.

CHAPTER VI

In the morning Mom took Billy up to the ranch, and I went along for the ride. Since I was sixteen, I had a day and night driver's license, but Mom didn't trust me with her car. Dad let me take the pickup most whenever I asked, but that was it as far as my driving went. Except, of course, for the tractor, but that was work and I tried to get out of it as much as possible.

Mom had a '72 Pontiac Catalina Station Wagon. She used it to haul kids, dogs, groceries, grain and what else needed to be hauled. President Carter called the car a gas guzzler and that made Mom mad.

"What does he know?" I heard her once say to Dad. "They elected the wrong brother president, that's what they did. Billy Carter should be in the White House. For all his beer guzzling, he's smarter than that jackass we have now."

Dad grinned and nodded. Mom kept talking. "I'd like to

see Jimmy Carter do in one of those little Jap-mobiles the work I do with that wagon."

Those were Mom's secret sentiments about the President of the United States. When Billy and I were around she didn't say anything.

It was a nice day. There were just a few clouds over the western mountains. It would be warm and not likely to rain.

At the bottom of the hill before going up to the gate, Mom put her gas guzzler into low gear. She didn't have to, but that was her way of driving. When we came to the gate I got out to open it.

We had two gates, a barbed wire and then a chain link. First we had just the chain link but that didn't last. Drunks, lovers, vandals and thieves edged up against the chain link with their cars and pushed it over. After that happened a couple of times, Dad put up a barbed wire gate. To push over the chain link, meant first a bad scratch. The night riders didn't go for that and we didn't have anymore busted gates.

I left both gates open. Mom and I'd only be a minute and we could close what we wanted on the way out. If I stood on my tiptoes and stretched my neck, I could see the tip of Zane Bodkins' smokestack. A wisp of smoke wafted up then disappeared in the breeze. The old man was home, sleeping off the effects of the night before.

Mom drove the gas guzzler down to the cabin. Tiberius was rubbing his fanny against a tree, trying to scrape off winter hair and dislodge a louse or two. He could scrape away his whole hide for all I cared.

Billy went down to take care of the bull, while Mom and I went into the cabin. Things looked all right to Mom, but not to me. The Judge had been drinking furiously, empty bottles littered the floor and every table. The Judge was sitting on the couch before the fire. He looked terrible, worse I'd ever seen him.

I leaned close to his ear. "What's the matter with you?" I whispered. "You trying to kill yourself?" That was a foolish thing to say.

The Judge looked at me through rummy eyes. He hadn't shaved and the salt-and-pepper beard made him look more miserable. He glanced at Mom then got up and went to the window. I followed him.

Billy had finished with Tiberius and was coming toward the house. When he saw my brother, the Judge acted like a madman. He doubled his fist, then went stamping about the cabin throwing bottles and glasses against the fireplace.

I thought about threatening to go get Janet Doris, then changed my mind. The Judge didn't look like he'd appreciate the humor. "What's the matter?" I asked, when mother had gone into the bathroom.

The Judge put his hands on my shoulder, and looked me in the face. For sure I thought he'd say something, but he didn't. He sat on the couch and buried his head in his hands.

Billy came in. The Judge glanced up, shook his head, then looked away. Mother finished in the bathroom and she and I left. We'd pick up Billy in the afternoon, when we came to feed.

I closed and locked the chain link fence, so sightseers wouldn't drive up, but left the barbed wire fence down. Against the western hills I could see the outline of a grey thunderhead. I'd been wrong about the weather. It could storm.

When we got home, I went to my room to change. Wee Willie slithered to a corner of the acquarium when I came through the door. "Go ahead," I said. "Move wherever you like. It's your privilege. You don't have long for this world. In another week you'll be pickled."

I put on a brown sport shirt, open at the neck, brown slacks and my tennis shoes; then went into the kitchen. Mom looked me over to see if I was presentable, frowned at the tennis shoes, then let me go.

As I passed the Conoco Station, Harold was chewing out Coot. I didn't get the whole conversation, but what I heard amounted to the fact that Coot was spending too much time washing the windows and inflating the tires of a certain young lady who drove a pink Chevy Impala. Although she came in several times a day for Coot's attention, not once did she buy any gas. "Probably fills up at the Independents," complained Harold. "Well then, let them clean her windows. You understand, Coot?"

Coot was understanding, but he wasn't liking. "Fine thing when a station can't give a little service, particularly to a pretty girl." He mumbled, wiped his greasy hands on his greasy overalls, then busied himself at fixing a flat. Harold went inside to explain to a customer that electronic ignitions don't have points.

A block past the service station, but on the other side of the street was the public library. Some people use the library for things other than books. Steely Marks was huddled in a corner of the foyer with Nancy Jo Dalton. Steely was wearing his black leather jacket, black pants and boots. Nancy Jo was dressed like Steely only she had on blue jeans. They were passing a cigarette back and forth.

I nodded to Steely as I went up the stairs. Steely didn't like to be interrupted when he was with Nancy Jo. He didn't look at me, only took a long pull on his Lucky. Nancy Jo turned and smiled in my direction. That made Steely mad and he choked on his smoke. I laughed and continued up the stairs.

For a jerkwater town, Pocatello has a good library. There are two floors. The ground floor is for kids. It has lots of books and a place set aside for story telling, pupppet shows, and children culture; stuff like that.

Upstairs was where I spent most of my time. It was divided into compartments without walls. There was a newspaper compartment where the town cheapies came to read last night's news. Another compartment held a group of painting reproductions which you could check out for a couple of weeks. "Instant culture," I called it.

In one corner was a photocopier. For a dime, if you pressed your face to the glass and kept your eyes closed, you could get a weird picture of yourself. I only did that when no one was looking.

The girl at the reference desk's name was Mary Flowers. I thought that was sort of sweet and funny. She wore a red and blue striped sweater and skirt, which looked good on her because she wasn't fat. She had short blond hair which she kept out of her eyes with one of those barrettes.

Mary Flowers had a little hump on her nose, but I didn't notice it much, because she had a nice smile, having had her teeth straightened.

I thought she was nice. She never kicked me out for whistling, like the old bat that worked weekends. When I forgot and started whistling, Mary would come over and touch my arm. "You're whistling, Davy," she would say. Then she'd smile pretty and I'd realize I was whistling and shut up.

"Here's your books, Davy," Mary said. She was holding a couple of books on reptiles for me.

"Thank you." I smiled real cool, then took the books and went over to a table near the windows that looked down on the parking lot. If I worked hard, I could finish my science project. I was doing a report on snakes.

According to the encyclopedia, some snakes have over three hundred vertebrae and associated pair of ribs. An estimate of the number of ribs in the living snake may be made by counting the scales along the snake's abdomen. One scale equals one rib.

The encyclopedia was accurate on that matter. I had verified their statements by counting the scales on a snake's abdomen, and afterwards mounting the reptile's skeleton.

The removal of the skin and flesh from the snake could have been an exacting and delicate operation. However, that task I left to others. To be precise, I left the job to carrion beetles, small brown and orange insects which subsist on dead flesh. Two weeks in a shallow grave under the ministry of those fellows left my specimen devoid of flesh. Afterwards I further cleaned the skeleton by boiling and then later submerged it in clorox which gave it a glistening white appearance.

Mr. Ravelli thought highly of my project and had me scheduled to attend the high school science fair in Boise. I had agreed to go, although I'm not fond of the state capital.

Still for Mr. Ravelli and the sake of science, I intended to go. The one to suffer most being Wee Willie.

You've met Wee Willie. He was my pet garter snake, undoubtedly a close relative to the mounted skeleton.

Wee Willie was four feet, six and one-half inches long. For several weeks he had to content himself with living in the small aquarium. I gave him a live mouse weekly on which to live. When I went to the science fair, I would pickle Wee Willie in a jar of formaldehyde. Mr. Ravelli felt the preserved snake next to the skeleton would be of considerable scientific interest.

In the library that day, I had only to finish the research and bibliography elements of the report, and the project would be completed.

I was about to record the number of metacentric and acrocentric chromosomes for Wee Willie's family, when I was distracted by a disturbance at the reference desk.

Russell Jones, Loretta Cager, Harry Echo, Buddy Bearpaw and a short swarthy man, whose name I was to learn was Henry Who-Walks-on-Moon, were demanding to see the library's collection of Indian books.

"In which Indians are you interested?" asked Mary Flowers. I thought the back of her neck looked pretty.

The question stopped the NOI leader. His only thought had been of his own band of Indian.

Mary Flowers read the perplexed look on Russell Jones' face. "Perhaps your interest lies with North American Indians," she said.

"Yeah! That's it. North American Indians," blurted Russell Jones.

"Then come right this way," said Mary Flowers. When they left the reference desk, I noted that Phil Snooper and his four thousand dollar Hasselblad lurked in the shadows.

"Sections 970.1 to 970.5 are collections pertaining to North American Indians." Mary Flowers pointed out the stacks. I watched the goings on from behind the green cover of an *Introduction to Herpetology* by Goin and Goin. There was a large number of Indian books. More than I would have cared to read.

Loretta Cager glanced nervously around the library. I doubt she'd ever in her life read a book without pictures.

Harry Echo was along for the political ride and he showed it, obviously bored. Buddy Bearpaw was almost sober.

Henry Who-Walks-on-Moon was aptly named. I'll tell you about him.

As the school board of district twenty-five was well aware, Pocatello High School had a significant drug problem. Rarely did a week pass without some glassy eyed kid climbing the walls. That was how Henry Who-Walks-on-Moon looked. "He's a hop head," I muttered to myself. "High as a kite."

"You don't have much written by Indians," Russell Jones grunted at Mary Flowers.

"We have everything they've written," Mary Flowers smiled sweetly. "If you know any Indian people, please encourage them to write. We'd appreciate learning about Indian culture from Indians themselves."

Russell Jones sulked. He'd been had. The library scene he'd planned for the benefit of his speaking engagement would not come off. He and his entourage were set to leave when Phil Snuder caught sight of me and whispered to the NOI leader.

Russell Jones came over to where I was sitting and leaned on the desk. He wore brown cowboy boots, blue jeans, and a white Tee shirt. Around his neck was a conch shell necklace like one I'd seen a gigolo wear in a movie.

Up close, I could see little scars about his eyes and forehead; merit badges from fights in the drunk tank and prison. I couldn't take Russell Jones, I knew that. In prison a guy learns to fight dirty. He would have had me before I got in one good lick. Even so, I stared back into his insolent face.

Loretta Cager came up beside Russell Jones and also stared at me. She had on a frilled brown leather skirt, same colored vest, a white full sleeved shirt, knee length boots, and no underwear. The woman was smallish in body and

57

interested me not at all. I don't think she interested Jones either because he elbowed her aside.

Henry Who-Walks-on-Moon came up beside Russell Jones. He was dressed similar to his mentor, Russell Jones, only around Henry's neck hung a large turquoise necklace that reached toward a brown navel which protruded through a hole in his shirt.

I could take Henry Who-Walks-on-Moon. I knew that. Only he was so far out, I'd have to cool him before he realized he was in a fight.

Harry Echo skulked in the rear behind one of the stacks. I do not remember how he was dressed and do not care. He had poisoned his son's mind against me, a disservice more to Andy than anyone else. I would never forgive him.

Phil Snooper and the four thousand dollar Hasselblad stood posed to snap pictures should anything of interest transpire. Buddy Bearpaw stood beside Snooper awhile and then came over to Russell Jones.

I kept looking at Russell Jones without blinking. This was a game I was well prepared to play, having never once been stared down in my entire life. I don't think Buddy Bearpaw realized I was the guy he'd leaned on a couple of days before in front of Nick's Place. But I remembered.

I let my hand curl around Goin and Goin's *Introduction to Herpetology*. Unfortunately it was a light book and could do little damage; yet it was all I had to defend myself and, if necessary, perhaps its sharp edge might be useful.

Russell Jones smiled at me. His teeth were all capped, thanks to the United States Public Health Service. His was not a friendly smile so I did not return it.

He should have had brown eyes, but they were grey. The eyes too were smiling as if they knew a secret that concerned me. I became afraid and in desperation felt like reaching up and taking Russell Jones by the throat.

"Davy, I'd like that book returned in a few minutes." Mary Flowers stepped up to the table and motioned toward the herpetology book. "Please terminate your conversation and finish your report." Pretty Mary Flowers to the rescue!

Russell Jones smiled more broadly at me, then turned and with his entourage left the library. I watched them go, then returned to my report. I could not finish it; I was too afraid. Afraid of a smile.

I returned the reference books to Mary Flowers. She reached across the desk and squeezed my hand. "Come back tomorrow Davy," she said. "Come early and stay late!"

"Thank you," I said and went out through the glass doors. Steely and Nancy Jo were gone.

At the service station, Coot was putting a dollar's worth of regular in his girlfriend's car.

CHAPTER VII

For lunch Mom made toasted tuna salad sandwiches and tomato soup. I had two sandwiches and two bowls of soup, plus several bread sticks coated with butter. This makes a pretty good meal when washed down with a glass of milk.

I figured Billy would be making himself peanut butter and jelly cracker sandwiches at the ranch with hot chocolate to drink. That was his way. He could always fix himself up something good to eat.

After lunch I changed into my work jeans, plaid shirt, and boots. Then I sat on the front porch and read a paperback I'd bought a couple of days before at the drugstore. The book was about a high school girl whose mother was a religious fanatic. The trouble was that the mother's religion didn't rub off on the daughter. The teeny-bopper spent her time lifting things with her mind. A feat of cerebration which later caused her and the community no end of trouble.

For a while I tried to stare at things and make them move, but with only limited success. I say "limited success" because once I thought I'd caused a blade of grass to move, only later saw an ant crawl out beneath the waving leaf.

At four forty, Dad and Uncle Al pulled up in the pickup. I hollered to Mom that I was going with them to the ranch to feed and pick up Billy, then jumped in beside Uncle Al. "How you doing, kid?" Uncle Al poked me hard in the ribs.

"Great, Unk!" I hit him back, hoping it was harder than he'd got me. Uncle Al laughed and let it go at that.

On the way up Jimmy Creek we passed three police cars. "There goes the tax money," said Dad. Over the protest of howeowners, the city had recently annexed the Jimmy Creek area. "The cops are out in force to show the people that they're getting their money's worth." He laughed to himself.

From the bottom of the hill going up to the ranch we saw half a dozen prowl cars and at least ten cops by the ranch gate. "Now what?" said Dad. He drove up the road slowly, glancing into the fields on both sides looking for any more Willie Echos.

The chain link gate had been smashed and lay dangling from its hinges. A police car blocked the opening between the two halves of the gate. To one side Abe Solomon stood talking to a guy in a brown suit.

Phil Snooper and his four thousand dollar Hasselblad were everywhere taking pictures. The reporter grunted with delight when he saw the three of us get out of the pickup. He shoved the camera in front of our faces.

"Get out of my way, or you'll be picking that box out of your backside," growled Uncle Al. Phil Snooper backed off, but not so far that he couldn't get a good picture of Uncle Al's snarling face. For a skinny twirp, the reporter had guts. I never would have dared pull half the stuff he did, especially with guys like Uncle Al.

"Now what?" Dad repeated to Abe Solomon what he'd uttered in the pickup. Most of the cops gathered around to hear the conversation.

"Trouble, Frank," said the sheriff. "A bunch of Indians busted through your gate and have taken over the place."

Dad was stunned. He looked at me in disbelief, then down the road toward the cabin. "Why?" he asked.

"Because they say they've reclaimed their land." The guy in the brown suit pushed his fat gut against Dad's chest. "They said they've had enough and they went in."

The guy in the brown suit was big, maybe six two, about the size of Abe Solomon, only where the sheriff was trim and athletic this guy was fat—fat gut, fat ass, the works. I could see a bulge near his left arm where he wore a shoulder gun.

"The guy's a slob," Uncle Al said to me. "Grease spots on his tie, a stubble beard, a crumpled brown hat, scuffed shoes, crooked nose, scarred cheek, carious teeth. The guy's a real slob." Uncle Al spoke loud enough so that everyone could hear.

"Who're you?" Dad looked into the face of the man who'd pushed up against him.

"This is Turk," interjected Abe Solomon. "He's the deputy United States Marshall for this area."

"What's he doing here?" asked Dad.

"It's sort of his province." Abe Solomon raised his hands helplessly. "A civil disturbance."

"Well how come you heard about this so soon and I didn't?" asked Dad.

"They called Snuder here," said the sheriff. He nodded toward the reporter.

"Who the hell are they?" Uncle Al elbowed Turk hard in the gut so he could get near the sheriff. The marshall glared and doubled his fist. Uncle Al glared back. He could take Turk, and the deputy marshall knew it.

"The NOI crowd," said the sheriff. "Russell Jones, Henry Who-Walks-on-Moon, Loretta Cager, Harry Echo, and Buddy Bearpaw."

"What do they want?" asked Dad. He ignored Marshall Turk and spoke to the sheriff.

"Your ranch," said Abe Solomon.

"I'll kill them," said Dad. He tried to push his way through the officers but was stopped.

"Take it easy Frank." Abe Solomon took Dad's arm. "Those people are armed and dangerous. We've got to use our heads. Let Turk here handle it."

"Shit!" said Uncle Al. He looked contemptuously at the marshall. "That tub would sell us out in a minute."

Turk's face reddened. He pulled a heavy black flashlight from his pocket, slapped it in the palm of his hand, and took a step toward Uncle Al.

Uncle Al laughed. "Easy tub," he said. "You'd look funny waddling around with that thing sticking out of your butt."

"Enough!" Abe Solomon stepped between Uncle Al and Turk. What good does talk like that do? We've got a boy up there to worry about."

"How is he?" Uncle Al turned from Turk to the sheriff.

"He's all right," said Abe Solomon. "We have radio contact with the cabin."

"The bastards are sure organized," said Uncle Al. "Tell them to let Billy go."

"I've already asked," said the sheriff. "They won't let him go until Frank signs over the ranch. That's their demand. They say it's not negotiable."

"I'll kill 'em!" Dad repeated. He didn't care that Phil Snooper's Hasselblad was in his face.

"You won't kill anyone!" Turk again poked his gut against Dad's chest; at the same time making sure his good side was exposed to Snuder's camera. "There's trouble here and I'm not sure who is right and who is wrong. Tomorrow Marshall Pete Marley will be here. He's an expert on these matters. For now, you come to your senses, get in your car and go home until I call you." He pushed Dad in the face.

Dad slapped the Marshall's hand away. "I'll kill 'em," he said again. "They can't take my land; I'll kill 'em!" Dad stood for a minute clenching his fists, then picked his way through the officers and got into the pickup.

"I'll kill 'em!" Dad repeated all the way down the Jimmy Creek Road and into our driveway.

CHAPTER VIII

Mom was waiting for us on the porch. By the look on her face, it was obvious she knew. And why not? It blared at us from the truck radio all the way back from Jimmy Creek. "Indians occupy McGrath Ranch. Indians reclaim ancestral ground. Billy McGrath hostage of angry warriors."

Mom looked at Dad a second, then rushed down the stairs and held me tight against her. I was a head taller than her but she reached up and patted my cheek.

All that hugging and patting was embarrassing but I didn't try to get loose. To her I was both Davy and Billy. She held on for life to what she had and I could feel her body shake with sobs. After awhile she let me go and we went into the house.

"Stay for supper?" Mom said to Uncle Al. Uncle Al nodded without speaking. He almost always stayed for supper.

Dad didn't wash, just sat at the table with his head in his hands muttering to himself.

Uncle Al and I washed up, then sat down while Mom brought in the food. "Ain't nobody going to talk?" I asked. I thought Mom or Uncle Al would say something, but they didn't.

Dad kept his face buried in his hands. When he was worried he liked to be left alone. "I'm like an old sick dog," he once said. "Let me crawl under the barn alone for a couple of days and I'll be all right." I figured he was way under the barn.

Mom had made spaghetti and meatballs. For greens we had asparagus spears. The others didn't eat anything and I didn't think I would either, but after awhile the spicy smell of the meatballs got to me and I took one. It was real good, but before I was half through Mom looked at me cross like. I hadn't prayed. I put the other half of the meatball down, and mumbled a hurried grace, then ate two more meatballs, then three more and a dish of spaghetti and two helpings of asparagus.

When I'd finished eating I went into the kitchen. Ordinarily Mom would have made me clear my plate from the table, but she wasn't paying any attention, so I got away with that.

Outside I heard the dog yelp. Duke was hungry. Billy usually fed him before supper. "That mangy cur can't wait a minute!" I grumbled.

I took the can of dog scraps from under the sink and went outside. Dad, Mom and Uncle Al still sat at the table staring at their plates not saying anything.

Duke didn't like me bringing his chow. He stood off and eyed me suspiciously. "Billy's not here, mutt," I said. "The Indians got him so you'll have to put up with me."

The dog didn't move. I slopped about half of what Billy usually gave him into his dish then went back inside. To heck with him!

The adults were still at the table staring at their empty plates. Uncle Al was talking. "We're going to have to ram the gate," he said. "If the Feds shoot, then we'll answer their fire. After that we go in and get the Indians." Dad looked at Uncle Al and rolled the idea over in his mind, then looked back down at his plate. Mom shook her head.

The phone rang. "I'll get it," I said. Mom started to get up thinking it might be some news about Billy, but I put my hand over the receiver. "It's some magazine guy from back East," I said. "Do you want to talk to him?" Mom shook her head.

The magazine guy said he'd heard on the radio about our ranch and the Indians and wondered if I'd mind answering a few questions.

"I don't mind," I said.

The guy asked me a lot of nosy stuff. How long we'd had the ranch, and who had it before us, and how big it was, and a lot more stuff.

I answered his questions, but really didn't feel it was any of his business. He asked me how old I was and I told him. Then he asked me if I had a girlfriend. I hung up on the jerk.

That was the first of the nutty calls. After that we had lots more. People seemed to call from every newspaper, magazine, and radio station in the country. A television guy wanted to send a crew to Pocatello to interview us. Mostly when they called and said who they were we just hung up.

"We ought to rip that damned thing off the wall," said Dad. Only he knew he wouldn't because that was the only way we'd get any news about the ranch.

Later Paul De Gamma called. He was Dad and Uncle Al's foreman at the steel car shop. When Mom heard who it was she got a little red. I'll tell you about Paul De Gamma.

Mom and Paul De Gamma had gone to school together and I sorta suspect at one time they had been more than just friends. Anyhow, Mom had married Dad and Paul De Gamma had never gotten married although at one time or another his name had been linked with almost every grass widow in town. My Dad called divorced ladies, grass widows. I guess that is an old saying.

Paul De Gamma was a good man. I'd met him and liked him fine. Dad and Uncle Al did too, and they talked a lot about him around the house. But whenever his name was mentioned Mom would try to put him down. Only she didn't put him down very hard, mostly about him not being married, and what she'd heard about him and the grass widows.

Mom also put Paul De Gamma down because his folks had been Catholics, yet she had never seen him in church. "He'll pay," Mom prophesied. "The Lord won't let his goings on go unnoticed."

I didn't say anything about that, figuring it was women's talk, and myself not being one to say what the Lord would and would not do. But I knew that the Lord never intended guys like Paul De Gamma to spend their life in a monastery.

The first thing I noted about Paul De Gamma when I met him was the way he smelled. He smelled like a man, nothing offensive, but like a man: sweat and muscle and man.

Paul De Gamma was six feet, three inches tall. He was dark complected with lots of curly black hair on his head and chest. He was a Portuguese.

The first time I met him he put his big hand on my head as if feeling gold in my red hair, then he laughed like he always did, showing his mouth full of white teeth.

Another thing Paul De Gamma was always doing was chinning himself. On door jambs, the ladders, on freight cars, anything that would hold his weight. He'd grab a hold then pull himself up a half dozen times. Well, I don't have to tell you he had biceps as big as basketballs. He ran the steel car shop and nobody gave him any sass.

That night Paul De Gamma called. "Heard on the radio about your trouble," he said. "Is there anything I can do?"

"No," said Dad. "And you needn't worry either Paul. We're going to get the ranch back!"

"I'm betting on it," said Paul. "But if you need any help you can count on me and the boys at the Steel Car Shop."

"Thanks," said Dad. "I appreciate your interest."

"That's all right," said Paul De Gamma. "And you don't

need to show up for work until you get this mess straightened out, Frank."

Dad hung up. "It was Paul De Gamma," he told Mom and Uncle Al. "Said we didn't have to go to work till things are back to normal." I could tell Dad felt a little better. Uncle Al grunted his approval. Mom didn't say anything. She was still a little red.

After the foreman called, I went into my room to work on my science project. I had a pretty good room, not too big, but big enough. There were two windows; one looked out on the alley and the other at the neighbor's garage. Mom had hung up drapes covered with old steam locomotives. I always felt she should have put them in her and Dad's room instead of mine.

In addition to my bed, I had a dresser and a stereo. The place was pretty crowded. There'd have been more room if I kept things picked up, but I didn't. Plenty of time for that later. "Why can't you be like Billy," Mom always said. Billy kept his room neat and his bed made. Well, I wasn't like Billy. I hoped the Indians would keep him until he got over his neatness and Mom got off my back.

Wee Willie was looking at me through the glass of his aquarium. Least ways I think he was looking at me. Who knows? Maybe he was asleep! Snakes don't have eyelids; instead, protecting their cornea they have a fixed transparent scale called a 'brille' that they shed with their skins. So like I said, who knows if he was asleep or not.

Up in the barn at the ranch I had a metal trap that caught mice alive. That night it was time for Wee Willie's weekly mouse supper. "Looks like your relatives screwed you out of your dinner," I said to Wee Willie.

The Shoshone Indians were also called the Snakes. Whether this was because they worshipped reptiles, or because of a wavy motion they made with their hands when referring to themselves no one has been able to explain to my satisfaction. So that night, I claimed they were Wee Willie's relatives.

I picked up three pairs of slacks from the floor and hung them over a chair, then straightened the covers on my bed. I was going to lay down on the bed and work on my report.

I thought about Wee Willie and his supper. "You'll have to make do with hamburger for awhile, old man," I said, then went into the kitchen to raid the ice box.

Uncle Al had gone. Mom and Dad were having an argument. Worst I'd ever heard. Mom was crying and carrying on about Billy. "My baby is up there," she sobbed. "I don't care about that ranch. I want my boy back!"

"Your boy is all right." Dad had Mom by the shoulders and was shaking her. "We're not giving up that ranch to no Communist Indians. Never! Never! Never! I've worked too hard!"

He let Mom go and sat staring at the supper dishes which were still on the table. Mom looked at him and didn't even try to catch the tears dripping from her nose. "My boy is up there," she said. "I don't care about the ranch, I want my boy."

"Shut up" said Dad. He looked like he was going to hit her, then changed his mind and grabbed the deck of cards and cribbage board from the center of the table. Then he looked to where Billy always sat and threw the cards on the floor. "Damn!"

I decided not to open the refrigerator and went back to my room. "You'll have to wait until morning," I said to Wee Willie.

Mom and Dad argued for some time, but I closed the door and pretended not to hear. I finished my report. "There she is," I held the papers up for Wee Willie's inspection. "In a couple of weeks we're off to Boise."

I undressed and hung my clothes in the closet. Billy would like that, I thought.

I put on my pajamas, turned out the light and got into bed. Billy always prayed before getting between the covers. I didn't.

The last thing I remembered was that Mom and Dad were still arguing. "Tomorrow I'm going to see Aaron Creech," said Dad. "The lawyer will have an answer. No Indian's going to take my land."

CHAPTER IX

In the morning I lay in bed waiting to hear Billy outside filling Duke's dish with fresh water. Then I remembered what had happened the day before. "Now I'll have to go out there and check that mutt's water," I grumbled. "Billy always has it easy."

From the kitchen, I could smell sausage and pancakes. Whenever Mom was sick, tired, or upset she made it worse by cooking an extra big meal. Made no sense to me. You'd think she'd rest, but she didn't.

I put on my best blue slacks and a blue long sleeve shirt. If Dad was going to see lawyer Creech, then I was going along. I glanced at the snake report on the dresser. "I'll hand it in tomorrow," I told Willie. "No school today."

Wee Willie was pressed close to the glass of his aquarium and I remembered that he was due to eat, so I went into the kitchen.

The radio was on and talking about the Indians up at

the ranch. But it didn't have anything new to offer so Mom turned it off.

Mom was like I knew she'd be, cried out and tired. She still was in her brown pajamas and over them the blue, down-filled bathrobe that Dad had bought her two Christmases back. On her feet were those silly half slippers that she favored.

"Any raw hamburger for Wee Willie?" I asked. "Couldn't get a mouse yesterday."

"There is some left over from the meatballs last night," Mom said.

I looked in the refrigerator. "There's nothing here," I said.

"What about that?" Mom pointed to a piece of cellophane wrapped meat on the second shelf.

"Oh!" I said. There wasn't much in the package, but more than enough for Wee Willie. I squeezed off half, made two little meatballs and took them into Wee Willie.

I put the meal in front of the snake's nose. His tongue flicked out a couple of times, tasting the air, but other than that he didn't move. I knew it was useless to wait around. He'll eat in his own sweet time. I went out to fill Duke's water dish.

The dog had plenty of water, but I emptied it out and ran in some new. "Fresh water twice a day," that was Dad's rule.

The sun was coming over the hills. It looked orange because it had to shine through the pollution from two phosphate plants north of town. "I bet Billy's been up for an hour," I thought. "If the Indians let him, he'll already have Tiberius watered and fed."

Once I was supposed to fill Tiberius' water trough only I forgot and the bull went a day without water. That snorty cuss liked to tear the fence down. Dad saw the empty water trough before I did and was plenty sore. "Slouching around again!" He shouted, and would have hit me with the brand he was carrying if I hadn't ducked out of the way. After that, Billy double checked to see if Tiberius had plenty of water.

Fifteen gallons a day, that's how much the bull drank. Three heavy five gallon cans worth, only you had to carry him four cans on account of evaporation. A gallon of water weighs eight pounds so that's one hundred and sixty pounds of water.

"Some day we'll put water right down into the corral," said Dad. But until that happy day comes, water had to be toted. Most of the time, I got Billy to do it.

Duke heard me at his water dish and started to wag his tail, then looked up and saw that I wasn't Billy, so he put his head back down. "Don't come over, you ungrateful mutt," I said. "Fill your gut with the water I pour and let it go at that. To hell with you," I muttered and went back into the house.

Dad was at the phone. He hung up and sat down at the table. "What time we going to see the lawyer?" I asked.

"How do you know about the lawyer?" Dad was dressed in his green suit. I thought he looked sort of funny, the way a guy looks who doesn't dress up very often, and doesn't feel comfortable. There were dark circles under his eyes and although he'd shaved, there were a couple of places on his chin where he'd missed.

"I heard you on the phone," I lied. I didn't want to let on that I'd heard him and mom arguing.

"Ten thirty," said Dad. He looked up to make sure Mom heard the time. Nobody said I wasn't going, nor anything about school, so I figured it was all set. It was only eight o'clock so Dad must have called the lawyer at home. That took guts! Never heard of a lawyer getting out of bed before ten.

"What did Mr. Creech say?" Mom set a plate of pancakes on the table, then forked on Dad's and my plate three sausages from a paper towel where they'd been soaking off grease.

"Not much," said Dad. "Said he'd heard on the radio about our problem and would be able to talk to us about it this morning at ten thirty."

"Hope he does more than just talk," said Mom. She didn't think much of Aaron Creech even if he had gone to high school with Dad and then graduated with honors from Stanford Law School.

"Don't you worry about Aaron!" Dad started to get angry again, then I guess he thought about all the arguing and fighting of the night before, so sat back down and poked his fork at a sausage. "I hope so too," he said.

Mom poured him some coffee, then stood next to him with her hand on his shoulder. "Anything else I can get you?" she asked, trying to make amends.

"No thanks," said Dad. "Sit down; don't worry. We'll get the ranch back."

"And Billy, too?"

"Yes, and Billy too," said Dad. He squeezed her hand.

I ate three pancakes and saw that nobody else was eating much, so took the last two on the plate, plus another sausage. We had two and a half hours before we went to the lawyer's office. No use waiting on an empty stomach.

When the time came to go, we piled into Mom's gas guzzler. Aaron Creech's office was only four blocks away. I was for walking, but Dad felt it would be more impressive if we drove.

Lawyer Creech practiced in a three story, fake marble-faced building on Third and Taylor Streets. The law business must be good, I thought, to be able to build a structure like that. The place was only three years old. On the corner was a sign saying: "Creech Building."

We couldn't find a parking place in front of the building, so had to pull around the corner. "Might as well have walked," I mumbled to myself.

Lawyer Creech's office was on the third floor. We took the elevator. "Aaron Creech, LL.D.," it said on the large mahogany door. "What does LL.D. mean?" I asked.

"Lawyer," said Dad. "Don't be stupid." He grabbed the brass handle on the door and pulled. It was the wrong way. The door swung in. Dad cursed, then pushed, and we entered Aaron Creech's suite of offices.

The reception room was magnificent: twelve foot high white ceiling crossed by oak beams, full length Indian Rosewood wall paneling, a red and black shag carpet. One whole wall was covered with certificates: Stanford University, the Idaho Bar, the United States Supreme Court, and a dozen others. Cheap advertising, I thought. Who is lawyer Creech trying to convince?

A young chick sat at a desk in the middle of the room. She was reading a confession magazine, and never looked up when we came in. Dad stood before her desk waiting to be recognized. He wasn't, so he purposely cleared his throat. The girl didn't move.

"Hello!" I said, plenty loud.

She stiffened, closed the magazine and raised her head. "Yes?"

We have an appointment with Mr. Creech," Dad said.

"Your name?" asked the girl. She had blond hair with black eyebrows and lashes. Above her overpainted red lips was a faint outline of black fuzz. Must be Italian, I thought. All Italian girls have moustaches.

"Frank McGrath," Dad said. "And family," he added nervously.

The girl glanced at an appointment book, which was mostly blank pages, then stood and went toward a closed door.

She had a slow, deliberate wiggle-waggle walk. Had to, I figured, so guys wouldn't notice her flat top.

She was behind the closed door a few minutes, then came out. "Mister Creech will see you shortly," she said to Dad. "Please be seated."

Dad said "thank you," and we sat on some chairs near the door. The girl returned to her confession magazine.

We sat a long time. I looked at my watch; it was eleven fifteen. We had been kept waiting forty-five minutes when a buzzer sounded on the girl's desk. She picked up the phone, mumbled "Yes," then turned to us and nodded toward the closed door. "Mister Creech can see you now," she said.

Aaron Creech's private office was even more elaborate than his reception room. There was the same beamed ceiling, paneling and carpeted floor, but the chairs were all stuffed and covered with a black velvet material. Pictures of Aaron Creech posing with dignitaries crowded the walls. I recognized the Governor, Congressmen, and a United States Senator.

Behind a large, hand carved, mahogany desk bobbed a bald head which belonged to Counselor Aaron Creech. The polished head was staring at some papers on the desk. Again Dad, Mom and I waited to be noticed.

What a place, I thought. You have an appointment, but still you wait. Then when you're supposed to be seen, they don't look at you. "Hello," I said, very loud.

Aaron Creech jumped. I guess he actually was reading those silly papers. He glared at me a second, then turned to Dad. A smile spread over the lawyer's face. "Why, Frank McGrath!" A pudgy hand was pushed across the desk. "Long time! No see!" He said.

Dad tried to smile, but was too nervous and didn't make much of a job of it. He shook Aaron Creech's hand, then introduced Mom and me. "This is my wife, Ellen," said Dad. He sort of pushed Mom forward. "And this here is my son, Davy."

Aaron Creech was a gnome in man's clothes. He was as tall as Dad, only built different. He had a flat head with the forehead pushed forward over bug eyes, long nose, and liver lips. He wore a dark suit of the same material as his office furniture—velour I think they called it.

The lawyer shoved a paw in my direction. I took it. The hand was moist and soft. I squeezed. Aaron Creech flinched. I could take you, lawyer guy, I thought. It would be easy!

I tried to hold the lawyer's eyes, but couldn't. He was ogling Mom. His lips parted revealing small widely spaced teeth. His pointed tongue darted in and out.

Mom looked away. She was not bad looking for an old lady in her thirties and had dressed stylishly in a grey knit suit with a white blouse and black shoes with a bow on the toe. The lawyer's attention embarrassed her.

Dad didn't notice about Creech and Mom. He was too wound up about the ranch. "Glad you could see us, Aaron," he said. "We're in a hell of a mess!"

"Yes, yes," Dad's voice brought the lawyer around. He sat down and waved us to chairs on the other side of the desk. "Heard about your trouble, Frank." His eyes hooked on Mom's blouse. The tongue worked his lips. "Tell me about it."

Dad told what had happened. Once he leaned forward and rested his elbow on the desk. Aaron Creech pushed Dad's arm away, then took out a handkerchief and polished where Dad's elbow had been. This done, the lawyer's eyes returned to Mom's blouse. Dad kept talking.

"So that's the story." Dad finished talking.

"I suppose you can prove the property is yours," said the lawyer. A smile tugged at the corner of his lips.

"Well everyone knows that's my place." Dad was rattled. He hadn't expected such a question.

"Of course we can prove it's our place!" Mom patted Dad's arm reassuringly, then looked at the lawyer.

"How?" asked Aaron Creech. He was amused.

"Easy," said Mom. She opened her purse and took out a stack of papers. "Warranty Deed, Title Insurance, tax receipts. What else do you need?"

She pushed the papers toward the lawyer. He glanced at them long enough to see that everything was in Mom's name. He pursed his lips thoughtfully. "I'm sure everything is in order," he mumbled.

"Sure everything is in order!" said Dad. "And we've got a little money too. We can pay for your services."

Aaron Creech grinned. He leaned back in his chair, and folded his hands over his abdomen. He had been unable to fasten the top button on his shirt.

"So you've got a little money," said the lawyer. "Tell me, Frank. You got a million dollars?"

"Come off it, Aaron," said Dad. "You know better than that."

"Well that's what you're asking for," said the lawyer. "A million dollar civil rights suit against the Indians. It would go all the way to the Supreme Court."

"Crap!" Dad doubled his fist, thought to strike the lawyer's desk, changed his mind and instead hit his knee.

"What about those monkeys?" He pointed to the pictures of the Governor and the United States Senator.

Aaron Creech grinned even broader. "They're part of the million," he said. "A big part!"

"Mister Creech?" Mom leaned forward on the lawyer's desk. He didn't try to push her off. "I've got a boy up there," she said. "I'm afraid for him. Can't you do something?"

The lawyer quit grinning. "I'm sorry," he said, and I think he meant it. "There's really not much I can do, but I'll try."

Mom and Dad looked at each other without speaking, then Mom put the ranch papers back in her purse and we left the lawyer's office.

The receptionist had her head buried in the confession magazine. "Goodbye," I said as we passed her desk. She didn't look up. "Friendly place." I slammed the door.

We drove past Nick's Place on the way home. Not much going on! I could make out only a couple of bucks at the bar; no squaws.

At Harold's Conoco, Coot was polishing his girlfriend's hub caps. Harold wasn't around.

We pulled into the driveway. Mom was crying. Dad was cursing the Communists. I couldn't tell if it was Communist lawyers, or Communist Indians. Probably both.

I went into the house with the folks, then thought about my Savage that needed cleaning. I took the rifle and some rags and oil from the closet and went back out on the porch.

I cleaned the outside of the gun first, then broke it down and started to work on the mechanism. The neighbor lady went by carrying a bag of groceries. She gave me a funny look. Thought it terrible that I had a gun.

We'd had guns in our family as long as anyone could remember. Pistols, rifles, shotguns, the works. Sort of a McGrath tradition. Dad said before long the government would put an end to it. "White Americans aren't supposed to have any culture," he said. "We're supposed to eat tacos and chitlins; count metric and turn our guns over to the Mafia, politicians and the rest of the crooks."

There were a few black clouds over the western hills. Maybe it would rain and maybe it wouldn't.

A car with California plates drove slowly past. The driver had his arm out the window holding up the roof. Everyone from California drives with his arm out the window. I think it's the law.

A woman with her hair in curlers sat next to the driver. She was his mistress. Dad said that "people in California don't get married anymore, only if they're the same sex." I think that's the law too.

The Californians stopped and stared at me. I stared back, made a face, then flipped them the bird. You know? Gave them the finger.

The driver got red. His mistress gasped. They drove away. "Keep going!" I said to their tail pipe.

The grass on our lawn was long for that time of year. Pretty soon it should be mowed, I thought. That's Billy's job. He can do it when he gets home.

I thought of Billy. He always gets the best of everything. Even now he's probably up there stuffing himself with ice cream and cake and playing it big with the Indians. Then when it's over and he comes home, he'll be a hero. So what! I thought. He won't be nothing to me.

Another car drove slowly past the house. I flipped them the bird too.

Duke came around to the fence and stood looking at me. He wagged his tail. First time he'd ever done that for me. I ignored him and went in to see if lunch was ready.

Mom and Dad were shouting at each other. Mom had the ranch papers out. "I'm going to burn them!" she said. "I'm going to get Billy back!"

Dad took the papers from her. "No bunch of Communists are going to take my land!" he said.

They quit fighting when I came in and Dad handed the papers back to Mom.

We had ham and cheese sandwiches and chicken noodle soup. I was the only one that ate anything.

The radio was on. Nothing new. The Indians were demanding their ancestral land. "It was non-negotiable," they said.

The governor came on and said as how the Indians were the first Americans and he was looking into the problem. "The governor is stupid," I said.

"He's a Communist," said Dad.

Mom looked down at her plate, dabbed at her eyes with a paper napkin, then went into the kitchen and started rustling around. We'd have another big meal for supper.

"When Al gets off work, we'll go up and see what's going on," said Dad. He left the table without eating, so I took his sandwich.

I went into the bedroom to see how Wee Willie was doing. He lay curled with his head under his tail. The hamburger was gone. I checked my papers for the science project. They were complete. "Tomorrow I'll take them to Mr. Ravelli," I said to Wee Willie.

I lay on the bed and read a book about a shark that swam around biting people in two, and outside of the people that were bitten, the only one that cared was the town police chief who couldn't do much about it because he didn't know how to swim.

A car horn sounded. I looked at the clock on my dresser. It was a quarter to five. That will be Uncle Al, I knew.

I went out front. Uncle Al was getting out of his car. He had a black Olds Toronado with wine-colored upholstery. It was a beautiful set of wheels. Cost him plenty.

Mom once said it was sinful to spend that much money on a car.

Uncle Al had grinned and said. "Sure it costs, but it really turns the girls on."

Then Mom got flustered and said, "That's sinful too."

I held the door for Uncle Al. "What's new?" he asked.

"Nothing," I said. "The shyster won't do anything without a million big ones."

"Figures," said Uncle Al.

Dad came into the living room. "How was work?" he asked.

"Okay," said Uncle Al. "Lots of talk about you and the Indians."

"What are they saying?"

"That it's a bum rap," said Uncle Al. "Paul De Gamma wants to get the boys together and run the damned Redskins not only off your ranch, but out of the country. 'Clear back to Mongolia where they came from,' " he said.

"I hope we don't have to do that," said Dad.

"You been up there today?" asked Uncle Al.

"No," said Dad. "I was waiting for you."

"Let's go," said Uncle Al. "We can take my rig."

We piled into Uncle Al's Toronado, I didn't see Mom, but knew she'd been listening.

CHAPTER X

We went right at the speed limit. Uncle Al already had two speeding tickets. One more and he'd be walking, so he was pretty legal, especially in town.

The road to the ranch paralleled for a couple of miles the railroad tracks. A string of freight cars had been pushed on to a siding. "Lots of red tags," said Dad.

"Why so many red tags?" I asked. The freight cars had red pieces of cardboard stamped to their sides.

"Bad order cars," said Dad. "Some heavy handed engineer has piled them up. They'll be pushed into the steel car shop for repairs."

"We're loaded now," said Uncle Al. "They'll have to be hiring some more men. Too bad you're not eighteen, Davy. I could get you on." He slapped me on the leg. It hurt. He meant it to.

"I'm going to college," I said. "You peasants can bang

your heads for peanuts against the side of a box car. I'll use my brains."

"Sure you will," said Uncle Al. He slapped my leg again.

There was a lone police car at the bottom of the hill which led up to our ranch gate. The policeman waved for us to stop. "It's Lazy Findly," said Dad. His name was Lazarus Findly, but people called him Lazy Findly. He was the town dog catcher but during busy times he got other jobs. Lazarus wasn't too sharp. Uncle Al went around him. Lazarus swore at us.

Near the gate was the usual half dozen prowl cars, plus Phil Snooper and his Hasselblad, plus a television outfit with a panel truck, plus a military vehicle that looked somewhat like a tank, only it wasn't.

"They've brought up an M-113, an armored personnel carrier," said Uncle Al.

"No," I said.

"What the hell do you mean, no?" demanded Uncle Al.

"It's not an M-113," I said. "It has a higher profile. It's an M-577; a command post carrier."

"You're a smart ass," said Uncle Al. I was right and he knew it. I'd seen it at the National Guard Armory.

"Hah!" said Dad. "Maybe we're getting some place."

A new guy in a blue serge suit was talking on a walkie talkie. The man was about Uncle Al's size and build, maybe a little younger. He kept his thinning salt and pepper hair in a crew cut. He should have done the same for his eyebrows. They were too bushy, almost covered his grey eyes.

I thought he should have worn glasses because he squinted when he looked at people. That made his pug nose wrinkle, and caused his lower lip to pull up in a snarl. It was obvious he was in charge. I didn't see Abe Solomon.

Dad went up to the guy in the suit. "Who are you?" asked Dad.

"I'm Pete Marley," said the guy. "United States Marshall for Idaho. Who are you?"

"I'm Frank McGrath," said Dad. "I own this ranch." He

pointed to Uncle Al and me. "This is my brother, Al, and my son, Davy."

Pete Marley glanced at us, then started to walk away. Dad stepped in front of him. "When are we pushing off?" asked Dad.

"Pushing off where?" The marshall was annoyed. He looked toward the bottom of the hill and Lazarus Findly.

"To run the Communists off my place!" Dad pointed at the Command Post Carrier.

"Hah!" said Pete Marley. He tried to turn away, but Dad grabbed his arm.

"What do you mean 'Hah'?" said Dad. "You've got the men and now you've got the equipment. Let's go!"

"We're not going anywhere," said Marley. "At least not now."

"Why not?" Uncle Al pushed his way up to the marshall.

"Because I'm not getting anybody killed," said Marley. He hated Uncle Al at first sight. I could tell that. Too much alike, I thought. Scrappers!

"Then why you got that M-577?" snarled Uncle Al.

"To make penetration of the perimeter impossible by those who wish to assume the role of meddlers, or vigilantes, or self appointed law enforcement officers," said the marshall.

"That's a pretty speech," I said. The marshall smiled. "It was the one given by the governor of Wisconsin at the time of the Alexian Monastery takeover," I added. The marshall snarled.

"Hah!" said Uncle Al. He spit at the Marshall's feet. Pete Marley was cool. He didn't let that bother him. "You seem to forget McGrath, that you've got a boy down there," he said.

"My boy is all right," said Dad.

"Is he?" said the marshall. "I wish I could be sure." He seemed concerned.

"Let's talk to them," said Uncle Al. "You've got that walkie talkie there. I suppose the Skins have one too. Tell them to put Billy on!"

85

"They won't," said the marshall. "I asked them."

"Bastards!" said Uncle Al. "Red bastards! And you marshall, you're yellow. We should go after them now!"

"I should punch your mouth, now!" Pete Marley advanced on Uncle Al.

The news media was having a field day. The television crew shoved microphones in everybody's face and Phil Snooper was snapping pictures.

Uncle Al stood his ground. "You're yellow, marshall," he said. "You didn't do anything at Wounded Knee. You didn't do anything at the Alexian Monastery, and the Indians know you haven't got the guts to do anything on Jimmy Creek."

Pete Marley was mad, real mad! But he didn't blow his cool. "Get him out of here!" He said to a deputy. "Get him out of here before I kill him!"

The deputy started to grab Uncle Al, then changed his mind. "Let's step over here," he said. Uncle Al grinned and walked over to the deputy's car.

I'd been watching things from up by the broken gate. Across the field, I saw a heat wave coming from the stack on Zane Bodkins' shack. The fuzz doesn't know it, but the old goat's up there, I thought.

Down the road from our cabin came the deputy federal marshall called Turk. He was naked except for his shorts and was pushing a grocery cart. I laughed out loud.

"What the hell!" said Dad. He was standing next to a television guy.

"He took food down to the Indians," said the television guy. "They made him strip down to his underwear."

"I'll bet they wanted more than groceries," said Dad. "Whiskey too!"

"They did," said the television guy.

"How much?" asked Dad.

"Plenty," said the television guy. He grinned.

"Crap!" said Dad.

A deputy brought Turk his clothes. "How were they?" asked the deputy.

"As usual," said Turk.

"Drunk?"

"Bombed! Especially that Bearpaw. He's crazy!"

"Did you see the kid?"

"No," said Turk. He sounded disappointed. "They've got him in the house."

"Anything else?" asked the deputy.

"The biggest, meanest bull I've ever seen."

"What's with the bull?"

"I don't think he has any food or water," said Turk. "He might go through the fence. If he does, watch out!"

I watched while Turk got dressed. "What you doing up here, kid?" Turk came up to me.

"Not running around naked," I said.

"Smart! Ain't you kid?" Turk reached for me, then backed off. The television crew was watching.

"Smart enough!" I laughed at Turk, then went over by Dad. "Mister McGrath are you ready to sign over your ranch?" asked the newsman.

"No!" said Dad.

"Not even to save the life of your son?" The television guy held the microphone real close. Dad got red, started to say something, then bit his lip and turned away. We got into Uncle Al's Toronado.

From down at the cabin we heard automatic weapon fire. "What the hell," said Uncle Al. "M-16's!" He started to get out of the car.

"It's all right," said a cop. "They been doing that all afternoon. Doesn't mean anything."

"Jesus," said Uncle Al.

Phil Snooper came up to the window and shoved his Hasselblad in Dad's face. Dad snatched at the camera but Snooper pulled back. The reporter pressed a button, and I could hear the camera snapping pictures in rapid succession.

We drove down the hill, Lazy Findly stood in the middle of the road so we couldn't get by. "What're you doing up here?" he snarled.

"Trying to look at my ranch," said Dad. "What're you doing?"

"My duty!" snapped Lazy.

"Crap!" said Dad.

Lazarus swore at us, but moved aside when it looked like Uncle Al might run him down.

When we got home, Mom was waiting for us at the door. She had the *News* in her hand. "What happened?" she asked. "How's Billy?"

"I don't know," said Dad. "I never learned a damned thing."

"The marshall's not sure Billy's all right," I said.

Mom looked pale then began to cry. "What does he mean, Frank?" She grabbed Dad's arm. "What happened to Billy?"

"Nothing!" said Dad. He brushed Mom away. "Like I told you, I never learned a damned thing. The kid is all right! Just some marshall lipping off."

"Is that right Davy?" Mom grabbed me by both shoulders and made me look at her. "What did the marshall say?"

"He said, he didn't know if Billy was all right, Mom. That's all. No more. No less."

Mom looked at me close to see if I was lying. She could always tell, then let me go and turned back into the house. Dad took the *News* from under her arm. "What's in the paper?" he said.

"Plenty," Mom mumbled. "Plenty!"

CHAPTER XI

The *Pocatello News* had missed the story of the Indian takeover the day before but they more than made up for it that issue. On the front page they re-ran the picture of Billy and me up by the gate. This time they had a circle around Billy's head. "McGrath boy remains at ranch," the caption said.

It seemed funny seeing Billy in the newspaper again. Him smiling like he had done when Phil Snooper took our picture. Seemed like a long time ago, only it was just a couple of days.

I wondered if Billy was smiling up there with Buddy Bearpaw. Billy didn't have any money now. Would Buddy Bearpaw still be his friend? I doubted it and began to feel a little sorry for Billy.

"What do you think of these headlines?" Uncle Al, like me, was reading over Dad's shoulder. "White rancher disputes Indian claim to burial ground." They read. Farther down. "Might makes right? Frank McGrath seeks land by force!"

"Newspaper people sure have a way with words," said Dad. It was a struggle for him to keep from tearing the paper to shreds. "They make it sound like we are the ones who are wrong."

"Maybe we are." Mom had come out on the porch. She was holding the ranch papers. "We don't own that land."

"We don't?" snapped Dad. "Then who in the hell does?"

"God!" said Mom. "That's who! The land is lent to us to use. We can use it for good, or we can use if for bad. The choice is ours, but in the end we have to answer to God. I say it's bad use when you'd rather have the land than your own child." Mom stared defiantly at Dad.

Uncle Al inched close to me. He didn't want in on the argument.

"The boy is all right," said Dad. He didn't sound as confident as before. "So what happens after we give them the ranch? Then they decide they want this house and after that your car. Where is it going to end? I supposed with the white people carrying their red asses around on their shoulders like Idi Amin of Uganda!"

Dad brushed past Mom and went into the kitchen. I heard him take a glass from the cupboard. "There's ice tea in the pitcher in the refrigerator," said Mom. She put the ranch papers on the table, and went into the kitchen after Dad.

I sat on the living room couch, and looked at the news. Uncle Al took the sports section and sat beside me. "Looks like we got a celebrity," I said. On the second page was a picture of Lance Buckner getting off a Western Airline. "Lance Buckner, star of numerous movies and hero of Alexian Monastery take over, rallies to Indian cause," read the caption.

"Don't look nothing like his movies." Uncle Al glanced at the picture. "Looks old as hell."

"Sure does," I said. The movie star had long hair tied in a bun at the back. He wore cowboy boots, studded blue jeans, vest and denim shirt. Around his neck hung one of those gawdy turquoise and silver necklaces that you see all over. "Got to have the turquoise necklace," I said. "Makes them look like a gypsy but they got to wear them."

Uncle Al laughed. "It costs money to join the club," he said.

"What's he here for?" I said. "Tell me that, if you can."

"Maybe he's going to jump on a motorcycle like in the movies and roar up to the gate and beat up the marshalls."

"Not the way he looks," I said.

"That's from too many of those Hollywood chicks," said Uncle Al. He elbowed me hard in the ribs. "They'll do it every time. Take heed, boy!"

"Take heed yourself," I elbowed him back.

"Supper is ready, Davy." Mom had come in from the kitchen. "You stay too, Al," she said. "We're having tacos."

"Don't mind if I do," said Uncle Al. He beat me to the table.

I had four tacos on my plate. I usually eat six tacos, but for starts, Mom had put four on my plate. Mom made her own corn tortillas, and they were good; soft, not hard like the shells you buy in the store. Also she made some flour tortillas kept hot by wrapping in a towel. The flour tortillas I spread butter on and ate like bread. To drink we had lemonade.

Uncle Al and I both ate four tacos, then made ourselves two more from the fixings on the table. I put a half spoonful of green chili sauce on my tacos. "You want some?" I pushed the jar toward Uncle Al.

"Hell no," he said. "That stuff will ruin your stomach!"

"Hah!" I said. "All the junk you pour into your gut and then complain that hot sauce would ruin your stomach. That's something I can't understand."

"Quiet Davy," said Mom. "Watch how you talk to your uncle." I shut up. Uncle Al grinned.

Mom and Dad didn't eat much. Dad ate half of one taco, then pushed his plate away. I don't think Mom ate anything. Neither of them looked good. The past two days they seemed to age a lot. That's what worrying does, I thought. Makes you look old fast. I'll never get old. I don't worry about anything.

Dad glanced at the cribbage board then jerked his head away. Mom looked too, only she kept her eyes on the board and cards, and twisted a handkerchief between her fingers.

I got up and gathered the plates, took them into the kitchen, and started loading the dishwasher. Billy was gone, so that meant I had to do the dishes. Then after that I'd have to feed Duke. I looked in at the dining room. Mom, Dad and Uncle Al were still at the table. Nobody gave a damn whether or not I worked myself to death.

I scraped the half eaten taco from Dad's plate into the dog dish. Duke would like that. I thought of Porky. Old Porky liked tacos too. But Porky was dead. Dad had killed him. "Someday you'll understand, Davy," Dad had said. But I knew I wouldn't.

"Tomorrow you have to go to school, son." Dad had come into the kitchen. He put his hand on my shoulder. "It's going to hurt, but you'd better go, and get it over with."

"Are you going to work?" I asked.

Dad thought a minute. "No," he said. "Not yet."

That's it, I thought. That's the way it always is.

I was going to go to my room, when the doorbell rang. Mom answered it. It was a woman. She was short, about Mom's size, and a little fatter. Only this lady was younger than Mom and she wore pants and a man's shirt, and had her brown hair cut short.

"Hi!" The woman said. "My name is Terri Johnson. I'm with the Sociology Department of the University. I would like to talk to your son, Davy."

Mom didn't say anything, only stepped aside so the lady could come in. If it was me that answered the door, I wouldn't have let her in. I would have said that Davy wasn't home. Cause I'd seen these people from the university before. They came to the high school to solve problems that didn't exist.

"My, what a beautiful bed spread!" Terri Johnson noticed the quilt that Mom had been working on in the living room. The quilt was almost finished and it was beautiful. A deep purple with a floral pattern and then a scarlet border. The quilt had taken Mom six months to do and was the best she'd done. I thought it was the best quilt anyone had ever done.

"You must be Davy?" The Terri creature caught sight of me looking from the kitchen door. Mom motioned for me to go into the living room. She thought that if anybody took the trouble to come see me from the university it must be for my own good. Mom didn't realize that sociologists were creeps.

"Come sit here Davy," Terri Johnson sat on the couch and patted a seat beside her. Dad looked in, couldn't see anything worth a damn, so went back into the dining room. Mom smiled at me, then went to join Dad. I was trapped! I sat down.

"I'd like to talk to you about your brother, Billy," said Terri Johnson.

"What about Billy?" I said.

"You tell me," said Terri Johnson. She had a hump in her nose, and brown cigarette stains around the nares. She didn't wear any lipstick. "I know it must be a strain on you, this Indian trouble and all. Tell me about it." She reached in her shirt pocket for a cigarette.

"Don't smoke," I said. "It really sets off my asthma. I turn blue!"

"Oh!" Terri Johnson put the cigarette back. I didn't have any asthma. Fact is even cigar smoke doesn't bother me a bit. But if you want to make the visits of the Terri Johnsons in the world short, tell them they can't suck on a cigarette.

"Do you sleep with Billy?" asked Terri Johnson.

"Yes," I said. It was a lie. "Billy and I, and Duke, and Wee Willie all sleep together."

"Duke and Wee Willie?" Terri Johnson was perplexed. She thought she'd done her homework well. Were there other McGrath children?

"Duke's our dog," I said. "And Wee Willie is my snake." I threw Wee Willie in as a phallic symbol.

93

"You're kidding me!" Terri Johnson said. She tried to laugh but it didn't come out too good.

I didn't say anything. Terri Johnson waited but still I didn't say anything. Terri Johnson got nervous, reached for a cigarette, then remembered my asthma and put it back.

She decided to abandon the bed kick. "Do you like Indians?" she asked.

"Miss Johnson," I said. "What do you want?" She was caught unaware by my question.

"Why, I want to help you."

"Are you writing a report, a paper?" I asked.

"Yes, I am." She decided to be truthful. "I'm going to make this interview part of my master's thesis."

I got up and went into my bedroom. Terri Johnson could answer her own questions. Wee Willie was looking at me from a corner of the aquarium. "What are you writing?" I asked him. "One thing about misfortune. It brings out people willing to make it worse for you."

I heard the front door close. Terri Johnson was going back to wherever sociologists come from.

I gave Terri Johnson enough time to be well away from the house, then went out to feed Duke. The dog wagged his tail when I came out the door and kept wagging even when he saw it was me and not Billy. That's a switch, I thought.

I filled his bowl and gave him some fresh water. He ignored the food and nuzzled my hand. "You're lonely, aren't you?" I felt that way myself, but wouldn't admit it. I didn't pet the dog, and then went inside. Uncle Al was still at the table drinking coffee.

The bell rang again. Probably Terri Johnson back, I thought. Dad went to the door. It was Father Bob Green from St. Vincent's Parish. Dad didn't say anything, just left the door open, and came into the kitchen. "It's for you," he told Mom.

Dad hated priests. Most of all he hated the bishop. That, too, came from the Vietnam War. "The bishop and priests preached, marched, wrote letters, gave money and did everything they could to assure that the Communists won the war," Dad said. "And then when it was over and the Catholics were slaughtered like sheep, the saintly Bishop raised his pious eyes and said, 'We'll pray for them!' Crap!" That's what Dad had said. "The Bishop is a Communist!" And Dad never went to church anymore.

Father Bob Green was a big, dark, husky man. He wore his nose plastered all over his face, a trophy from the two years of pro football he'd played before deciding he'd rather grapple the devil than the Packers. I didn't think I could take him.

Father Bob was old-fashioned. He wore a Roman collar, a black suit; the works. If he had ideas about politics, he kept them to himself. His sermons were about love, honor, decency and how you play the game. Dad would have liked Father Bob, only the priest came to St. Vincent's after the Vietnam War and after Dad had decided that all priests were Communists. So they had never spoken.

"Ellen, I'm sorry; real sorry!" The priest told Mom.

Mom tried not to cry, but she did. "I'm scared for my boy, Father," she said. "Real scared!"

The priest didn't say anything. He sat beside Mom on the couch and let her cry it out. I came in and sat in Dad's chair. Then we said the rosary for Billy's safety. I could have ducked out, but I didn't.

When Father Bob left, mother had quit crying. I think she felt a little better. Uncle Al poked his head around the door to make sure the priest was gone then came into the living room. "Those guys always make me feel uneasy," he said.

"Guilty?" I said.

"Shut up!" Uncle Al said. He meant it. I went back to my room.

I gathered the papers for my science report and put them in a blue binder. The papers looked the same only they didn't feel the same; like they'd changed. "Here it is," I said to Wee Willie. "The report that will rock the scientific world. In two weeks we'll deliver it in Boise."

Wee Willie, coiled in a corner of the aquarium, contemplated me with his usual cold look. "Too bad you're going to be pickled," I said. "You'd like Boise. You have lots of relatives there. The place is a nest of snakes."

I thought of Billy. How long had he been gone? Two days? It seemed longer. For the first time I was afraid for him. He'd probably laugh if he knew how I felt, I thought. Then I was mad at myself.

I kicked off my shoes, dropped my clothes on the floor and crawled into bed. Tomorrow was school again. After breakfast I'd walk over and pick up Steely Marks. He could fill me in on what I'd missed.

CHAPTER XII

Rain hitting against the window, wakened me. I looked at the luminous clock on the dresser, 5:00 o'clock; it was still dark.

I opened the window and looked out. It was a light rain, small drops. I tried to see stars around the edges of the clouds, but couldn't. No wind either. That meant the rain could last two or three days. I stuck out my tongue and tried to catch some drops but couldn't.

They'll need a big fire up at the ranch, I thought. The cabin was drafty and required lots of heat. I tried to remember what Billy had worn to the ranch the day of the take-over, but couldn't. Anyway I had a wool army shirt up there that Uncle Al had given me. Billy could wear that.

I closed the window and went back to bed. "Better get up Davy, it's seven." Mom woke me. I looked out the window. I had been right. It was still raining.

They'll be watching me at school, I thought. So I'll give

them something good to look at. I put on a long sleeved wool shirt. It was grey. Then I put on the pair of jeans Mom had bought me the week before. They were bells and had a flower on the hip pocket. I'd seen the price tag. They cost twenty-five dollars.

Mom had made strawberry crepes for breakfast. Crepes are those thin French pancakes. She'd filled them with strawberries and cream then rolled them up, and put more strawberries on top. I ate four.

"Pretty fancy breakfast," I said.

"Pretty fancy boy," said Mom. She poured more hot chocolate into my cup. "Hot chocolate goes good on a rainy day." Mom tried to smile but it didn't come out. She was too tired.

"We got hot chocolate up at the ranch," I said. "I'll bet old Billy is drinking some right now."

"I hope so," said Mom. "God how I hope so!" She sat down and her hand went to the pocket of her housecoat. She'd be fingering her rosary beads, I knew.

Dad didn't come into the kitchen for breakfast. Mom took him a cup of coffee into the bedroom. I picked up my report on reptiles, wrapped it in cellophane, then stuck it inside my shirt. Wee Willie was stretched out in the aquarium looking at the rain through the window. "Take it easy," I said to him, then put on my jacket and went out the back door.

The rain made it seem colder than it really was. The thermometer Dad had at the corner of the house read fifty degrees which wasn't bad for that time of year.

Duke came around the house and would have nuzzled my leg only I put my foot out so he couldn't reach me. Didn't want his wet nose against my Levis. He stood and looked up at me. I opened the gate and went out. "Take it easy," I told him. "Everybody take it easy, Wee Willie, Duke," I looked off toward the ranch. "Everybody!"

I tried to catch some rain on my tongue as I walked, then quit when I saw Coot watching me from the station. He probably thinks I'm crazy, I thought. Maybe I am. I sure as hell don't feel like much today.

There was a puddle on the walk in front of Steely's house. I jumped over it and landed on the porch. His doorbell was broken, so I knocked. Nobody came for quite awhile. I saw the curtain on the living room window part, and an eye looked out at me, but I pretended not to notice. Finally Mrs. Marks came to the door.

I knew before I saw her what she would have on. She wore an old torn red bathrobe and had her hair in curlers. That was her costume. When we came from school in the afternoon she'd still have on the bathrobe and her hair in curlers.

"Is Gregory here?" I asked.

"No," she said. "He's already gone."

"Oh?" I said. Inside I could see Steely sulking and looking like a guy who had been pushed into a fight but didn't really want any part of it.

Mrs. Marks saw me looking at Steely. "Now look here Davy McGrath," she said. "You run along. We're good people and don't want any trouble."

I looked again at Steely then at Mrs. Marks without saying anything. The way I saw it was that if she took the trouble of telling me that she was 'good people,' then that implied that I wasn't.

I went down stairs, splashed through the puddle and walked another block, then stopped. If my best friend thought I was 'trouble,' then it'd be worse at school.

I took the reptile report out of my shirt and looked at it.

"Reptiles of Southeastern Idaho," was the title I'd given it. "So what?" I said out loud. "So what!"

The paper slipped from my hand and fell in the gutter. I watched it float toward the storm sewer, then picked it up and went home.

When I got to the house, Dad and Mom were sitting at the kitchen table. The food before them was uneaten. Coffee sat cold in their cups. They were fought out; sat staring at each other without saying anything.

Mom looked at me. I anticipated her question. "It's no use," I said. "I got half way to school, then realized it was no use."

"No use." Dad mouthed the words silently and half grinned. "No use!"

I went into my bedroom and closed the door. Wee Willie was still watching the rain. "You've had a reprieve," I told him. "No Boise. No nothing! As soon as this mess is over I'm taking you up to the ranch and letting you go." I threw the reptile report into the wastebasket.

Wee Willie didn't look at me. He'd heard big talk before.

I stayed in my room and read a book I'd gotten from the library. It was about a coal mining family during the last century in Scotland. They had lousy jobs, lousy houses, and lousy pay. The only thing not lousy about their lives was the field where they played soccer. In the end, even that was taken from them.

"So other people have problems too," I told Wee Willie. "And maybe the good old days weren' so good either."

I heard the front door close and Mom's gas guzzler start up. I went into the kitchen. Dad was still at the table. "Where did Mom go?" I asked.

"She didn't tell me," said Dad. "Probably the ranch."

"Probably," I replied. Mom had stayed at home long enough. She'd want to see for herself what was going on.

I poured myself a cup of coffee, and sat across from Dad. He looked at me, then the coffee but didn't say anything. "What do you think?" I asked.

"Think? Crap!" Dad fairly shouted at me, then caught hold of his temper and said nothing. He was wound tight and would explode if pushed. I shut up and sipped at my coffee.

An hour later, Mom came home. She'd worn her best dress and coat. They were a dark blue color. The dress had a red rose design. The silly little navy cap that went with the outfit was soaked from the rain. Mom put her coat on a hanger and hung it on the door. She put the cap on the table. I tried to hide my coffee cup between my hands, but she saw it, and took it away.

"What's new at the ranch?" I asked.

"They didn't want to let me up there," she said. "That

Lazy Findly was down at the bottom of the hill and tried to shoo me away."

"Did you shoo?" I asked.

"No," she said. "I got out of the car and walked right past him. He did a lot of shouting and threatening but I ignored him and went up to the gate."

Dad grinned. He could picture in his mind what had happened.

"Poor Lazarus," I said. "Nobody pays him any attention."

"Anything at the gate?" asked Dad.

"Nothing," said Mom. "The officers were real nice, but couldn't say anything. 'Nothing to do but wait and hope,' said Officer Marley. I think he's in charge."

"That's a nice one," Dad growled. "Anything else?"

"Some shooting down by the cabin," said Mom. "Sounded like a machine gun, but Officer Marley said it was only an M-16 rifle and not to worry about it. 'Just the Indians making noise, he said.'"

"How's old Tiberius?" I asked.

"Bad!" said Mom. "I could hear him bawling and snorting even at the gate. Officer Marley said that the bull needs water, and if he doesn't get some soon he might go through the fence."

"I hope he does," said Dad. "And I hope he takes a bunch of red Communists with him when he does."

"Anything about the kid?" Dad asked. It was the first time he'd asked about Billy.

"No," Mom swallowed hard. "Nothing! Mr. Marley said the Indians haven't let anyone talk to Billy since they took over."

Dad put his cold cup of coffee to his lips, tasted it, then walked over and dumped it down the drain and poured himself a fresh cup. Then sat down again. "They can have the damned ranch," said Dad. "The Indians can take the whole thing. I want my boy back." He looked at Mom and smiled for the first time in three days.

Mom smiled back, then jumped on Dad's lap and kissed

him; not a little kiss either like married people are supposed to give, but long and hard; almost obscene.

It was noon and I was hungry. Mom didn't act like she was in any hurry to cook anything. He wasn't even back yet, but already Billy had goofed up my chow. I wanted to be mad, but couldn't.

"I'll get the ranch papers!" Mom jumped off Dad's lap. "We'll go get Billy right now."

"I don't know if it will be that easy," said Dad. "Seems to me a lawyer or a judge might have to rule on it or something so that it's legal. I expect the Indians will demand it."

"I guess you're right." Some of the joy went from Mom's face. "It'll have to be done legal. But by whom and how'll he get in touch with the Indians?"

"What about the reporter, Phil Snooper?" I said. "He started the whole mess. Seems like he should be able to finish it."

"There you go!" said Dad. "That would probably be the fastest way all around." He looked up the number in the telephone book, then dialed the *News*. "I'd like to talk to Phil Snuder," he told the person on the other end of the line.

Of course Phil Snooper wasn't in. "Well, this is Frank McGrath," said Dad. "You try and get hold of Snuder and have him call me. Tell him I've got a hell of an important announcement to make."

"I'll bet that won't take long." Dad winked and grinned at Mom when he hung up the phone. She grinned back and they went again to hugging and kissing.

As Dad said, it didn't take long. The phone rang. Dad took it. Snooper was calling.

"This is Frank McGrath," Dad said. "I've decided to give the Indians the ranch. No conditions. No exceptions. The whole thing, house, cattle, equipment, even the mortgage. All I want is my boy back."

There was some talk then Dad hung up. "Snuder is going to take care of it," Dad said. "Said it would take time, at least till morning."

"That long?" asked Mom. "I was hoping to have Billy

home tonight. I was going to cook Mexican Bake Dish. It's his favorite."

"We'll have to wait," said Dad. "Funny that Snuder didn't sound glad to hear about what I told him. Acted disappointed that it was over."

"Let him be disappointed," said Mom. "I don't care." She went back to sitting on Dad's lap and kissing him.

Then she and Dad started making plans. "We'll take a vacation," said Dad. "I got that week coming that I was going to work on the corrals. We'll take the boys and go to California—Disney Land, Knox Berry Farm, Sea World, the works." He was laughing at the thought of the fun we'd have.

"What about school?" said Mom.

"To heck with school. Let the boys miss a week. For Davy it won't make much difference and Billy doesn't care."

"You know how long since we've had a vacation?" Mom laid her head on Dad's shoulder.

"Never," said Dad. "We never had one since we got married. First it was the kids, then the ranch. Well, that's over. From now on we're going to enjoy life a little. And there's things around here that need taking care of too." He looked at the walls in the dining room that for years he'd intended to panel.

I went into my bedroom. Wee Willie was coiled in the center of his tank watching a fly walking around on the outside. "It's back to school in a week," I told him. "You don't need to worry though," I said. "I've dumped the science project for good. You're a free man as soon as we ransom Billy. Only you're not going to the ranch. Tomorrow we'll have no ranch."

I turned the radio on, expecting to hear a news flash that the McGraths had acceded to the Indians' demands. There was no announcement. Snooper's waiting for the evening news, I thought; a big scoop for the investigative reporter.

It didn't come out in the evening paper. For all anyone could tell, things stood the same. "You know what I think?"

I said to Dad and Mom at supper. "I think that Phil Snooper is sitting on the story of us giving up the ranch."

"Why should he do a thing like that?" My folks were so busy making plans they only half listened to what I said.

"So he can sell it to one of those big newspapers or television outlets."

"Hah!" Dad didn't think much of my argument. With one hand he waved me down, and with the other stuffed an onion ring in his mouth.

Mom had cooked steak with onion rings. She cooked the onion rings in beer, and they were real good. The alcohol boiled off, but they still had a beer taste and smell. Usually I ate several handfuls with my steak, but that night I let them sit and left the table.

"Where you going, Davy?" Mom asked.

"Not hungry," I muttered and went to my room.

"He ain't coming," I said to Wee Willie. "I can feel it. Billy will never come home again."

CHAPTER XIII

I went to bed early, trying to hurry the night along, but I didn't rest much.

The Judge came and stood at the foot of my bed. I was surprised. It was the first time I'd seen him off the ranch. "Hey Judge," I said. "You in the wrong place? Janet Doris isn't here."

The Judge was real agitated. He wanted to talk to me only didn't. Instead jumped from foot to foot. "Judge," I said. "You look like hell. You trying to match booze with those Indians up there? Forget it man! You never can do it!"

The Judge again started to talk; stopped as if he was listening to something, then gave up and went away. I tried to sleep.

Uncle Al came over late in the evening. I could hear

him and the folks talking and laughing in the kitchen, planning what they were going to do when Billy came home. I put a pillow over my head to shut out the noise.

CHAPTER XIV

It was near morning. I could tell by the grayness that filled the room. I was awakened by someone pounding on the back door. I put on my bathrobe, went into the kitchen, switched on the light then opened the door.

Zane Bodkins was the pounder. He looked as rough as I'd ever seen him. He shook all over from want of a drink, and his false teeth chattered from the cold. He blinked several times to get used to the light, then his eyes surveyed the room, hoping to see a bottle. "I gotta see your dad, Davy," he said. "Gotta see him right away!"

I didn't have to get my Dad. He and Mom had also been awakened by the pounding and came into the kitchen. Zane Bodkins looked over my shoulder at Dad. "They shot your boy, Frank," he said. "They shot him bad!"

Right then I felt sick like I was going to throw up. I wanted to run into my room and let it be night again, and let it be that Zane Bodkins had never come.

"He dead?" asked my Dad. Dad was behind me but I could tell he was looking hard at Zane.

Zane didn't say anything. He looked at the ground and nodded.

I stood with my back to the folks. I heard Mom sink into a chair and start sobbing.

"How'd it happen?" asked Dad.

"It was just before dark," said Zane. "That Tiberius bull of yours had been acting up bad all afternoon. Hadn't had any water in three days, you know. Then I heard boards breaking and knew he was starting to bust out of his corral, so I snuck down for a closer look.

"The bull was busting out all right. Had taken one two-by-ten in the middle and was fixing to take another one.

"The Indians was whooping and laughing in the cabin. I don't think they even knew what was going on. Then that Billy Boy of yours came sneaking out a window, went to the faucet and filled a bucket and headed for the bull. It was then he got it.

"By who?" demanded Dad.

Zane hesitated a minute like he didn't want to mention names, then his eyes met Dad's. "By Buddy Bearpaw," he said. "Buddy came staggering out of the cabin with one of those fancy army guns. He looked at your boy, didn't say anything, just pulled down and shot him."

"The boy went down hard; didn't cry or nothing, just went down. Then that crazy fool did the same thing with the bull. Shot him dead!"

"Why didn't you come sooner?" Dad's voice broke and the question came out in a whisper.

"I wanted to, Frank," said Zane. "You can believe that, but I figured after the shooting the marshalls would come down the road. I waited, but they never came."

"The other Indians came out of the cabin. That big guy was mad as hell. He punched Buddy real hard several times. The squaw was crying. She picked your boy up and took him inside. After that I could hear them all fighting.

"I came as soon as I could, Frank." Zane's eyes explored

the room. His tongue flicked across his lower lip. "You believe I came as soon as I could?"

"I believe you did," said Dad. He went to the cupboard and took the bottle of Old Charter he saved for entertaining. "Take this, Zane."

Zane caressed the bottle of whiskey, started to open it but didn't, then cradled it under his arm, and stumbled out into the dawn. "Thank you, Mr. McGrath," he said. "Thank you."

I watched Zane Bodkins stop at the corner of the house, fumble with the cap of the bottle until he got it off, then drain a third of the whiskey. This done he recapped the bottle, tucked it under his arm, and went through the gate. Duke stood to one side watching. Zane went toward town.

I turned and saw Dad looking at me. Only I knew he wasn't seeing me, but Billy. Dad's eyes were squinted up like he was in pain, and a low hurting sound came from deep in his gut.

Mom was still crying. Dad glanced at her, then looked away. He acted guilty and ashamed. That was his way. He blamed himself for everything that had happened.

Still with that hurting sound coming from him, he went to the phone and dialed. The phone rang for several minutes before Uncle Al's sleepy voice answered. "They shot Billy," said Dad. Uncle Al said something that I didn't hear. Dad said, "Now!" Then hung up.

I followed Dad into the hall where he took his 30-06 and a box of shells out of the closet. I reached for my Savage. Dad put his hand on my arm. "You stay with your Mom," he said.

I ignored him and took the gun and a box of shells. Out front, I heard Uncle Al's car drive up.

It was still dark enough that we could have used the porch light, but nobody turned it on. Dad motioned Uncle Al toward the pickup. Uncle Al was carrying his 7 mm Remington. I got in between Dad and Uncle Al. No one said anything.

Before we left, Mom came down the steps and stood beside Dad. She put her hand behind his neck. "Frank."

109

She said. Then turned his head and kissed him. Dad looked more ashamed. He put the truck in reverse and we pulled out of the driveway.

A red tint at the peaks of the western mountains slowly descended into the valley. However, it would be another hour before the sun would be seen coming over the eastern hills. We drove silently through the grey streets. Dad should have turned on the headlights, but didn't. Neither Dad or Uncle Al spoke. I held Dad's Browning between my knees and the Savage near my right leg. The guns felt cold. I ran my hand the length of the Savage. It made no difference, the weapon remained cold and impersonal.

I thought about Billy and how it didn't seem real that he was dead. And I thought about where we were going and what we planned to do. I wasn't scared or anything, only a little curious as to how we were going to get by Pete Marley at the gate.

I wasn't mad at the Indians not even Buddy Bearpaw. It was like I had to go do a job and didn't care one way or the other about it. I thought about the automatic weapons the Indians had, and how they sounded, and that I might be killed. I didn't care about that either. I rubbed my hand again down the length of the Savage. The gun remained cold.

I looked at Dad. He stared straight ahead. I saw the white of his knuckles where they gripped the wheel. He still had that hurt sound coming from deep in his gut.

I'd once heard a sound like that come from a badger I'd killed. It was late in the evening. I was hunting with a 22 rifle and had caught the animal away from its den.

My first shot took him unaware, had spun him around and then he'd started with that deep grunting sound. I was standing near his hole so he came straight at me. I kept shooting him and with each hit he gave that grunting sound, but kept coming. He'd been only two feet away when I'd finally hit him between the eyes, and laid him down for good.

Uncle Al was nervous. He kept sticking his little finger

in the muzzle of the Remington. Several times he checked his jacket pocket to be sure he had his bullets.

We turned onto the Jimmy Creek Road. There was a light on in the kitchen of Mrs. Smith's house. I looked at my watch: 6:10 a.m. If you've raised chickens for sixty years, and gotten up with them all that time, I guess you don't shut the habit off all at once just because some man at the Social Security Office says you're retired.

At the bottom of the hill, Lazy Findly was asleep in his car. We went around him without any trouble. Lazarus never woke up.

In the half light, the command vehicle loomed large and forbidding. Two deputies leaned against it drinking coffee. More officers dozed in their vehicles.

One of the men by the command vehicle looked our way as we came up the hill, thought us another police car and continued with his coffee.

As we got nearer, the man looked up again, recognized the pickup and motioned us to the side.

Dad ignored him and slammed on the accelerator. The old pickup kept its speed. When the deputy saw we weren't slowing he began waving and shouting. Men piled from their vehicles, some dragging guns after them. I saw Pete Marley and Phil Snooper poke their heads out of the command vehicle.

A hundred yards from the fence, about the spot where Willie Echo had been found, Dad turned into the field. The pickup bounced across gopher holes and I had to put my hands against the ceiling to keep from banging my head.

The police were all shouting now, some honked the horns of their cars. Maybe they thought we didn't hear them.

Dad took the fence at one of the posts. The Chevy slowed a little, then the barbed wire snapped and we went through. I slunk down, expecting the police would open up on us. They didn't. We drug wire on the bumper for awhile then it fell loose and we went around the corner out of vision from the gate. Ahead I could see the cabin.

"Let me out at the corral," said Uncle Al. Dad slowed;

Uncle Al jumped out, vaulted the fence on one hand, then ran in a crouch and flopped down behind Tiberius. The bull was on his side, his legs sticking straight out. He'd begun to bloat.

Dad drove the pickup just beyond the house, then hit the brakes. "Behind the posts, Davy!" He said. We left the truck and ducked behind the two stacks of fence posts that I'd neglected to move. Dad took the pile nearest the barn. I was between him and Uncle Al.

From inside the cabin I could hear the Indians shouting and quarreling. They hadn't seen us drive up.

After awhile someone looked out the window. Dad was watching through his scope and could have picked the guy off easy, but didn't. Then there was more arguing inside. I heard a radio crackle.

Pete Marley's voice came across. The Indians had him on their C.B. radio. I couldn't make out what he told them, but after awhile an arm waving a white undershirt poked out the window. Russell Jones opened the door and stepped out. He was unarmed and wanted to talk.

Dad looked at me, then at the corral. Uncle Al shook his head. Dad got up anyway, laid his Browning against a post and went toward the NOI leader.

They didn't meet. Dad was half way to the cabin when someone opened up from the window. Bullets danced around Dad's feet, then he hunkered up and backed toward the fence posts. A red spot that grew rapidly larger stained his shirt just below his chest.

Dad grabbed his gun and ducked behind the posts. Bullets kept raising little puffs of dust in front of us. Some made a whacking sound as they hammered into our barricade. I pushed my face into the dirt.

Russell Jones was real mad. When the shooting started he turned toward the cabin shouting and shaking his fists. He was running to the window where the firing was coming from when Uncle Al's 7 mm slug tore the Indian's head apart.

The firing stopped. The guy in the window hadn't known about Uncle Al.

Nothing happened for several minutes. I could hear Pete Marley's voice shouting from a radio in the house, but no one was answering him.

I looked at Dad. He was laughing the way he did when he'd been hurt bad. He caught me watching him and winked. The gesture was meant to reassure me. It didn't. Dad's face was pain. A pool of blood formed beneath his abdomen.

The door opened a little. A hand stuck out waving the white shirt. Dad watched it through his scope. He figured where the body stood that was waving the flag. He squeezed off three fast shots. I saw the wood door splinter. It swung open. Loretta Cager fell onto the walk. She was dead.

Dad took the clip out of his gun, reloaded, then pushed it back into place. He was wheezing; having trouble getting air.

The cabin was quiet for several more minutes, then the Indians did a crazy thing. Screaming and shooting they rushed the door.

First was Henry Who-Walks-on-the-Moon, then Harry Echo. They went down in the middle of the walk. I could hear Dad's and Uncle Al's bullets digging into their bodies. I didn't shoot.

Last came Buddy Bearpaw. He tried to run but lurched in drunkenness. He got past Harry Echo and Henry Who-Walks-on-the-Moon, then stood staring stupidly around.

I looked at Dad. His face was in the dirt. I couldn't see him breathe.

Uncle Al crouched on one knee. He was frantically clawing at the breech of his 7 MM. It had jammed.

Buddy Bearpaw's eyes focused on the corral. He put his M-16 to his shoulder and pulled down on Uncle Al.

I watched Buddy Bearpaw through the peep sight on the Savage. I wanted to help Uncle Al, but couldn't force myself to do anything.

Then in the door, I saw the Judge. He was shouting. "Shoot, Davy! Shoot!" he said.

I jerked the trigger on the Savage. I wasn't holding the

gun tight enough. It pounded my shoulder and head. For a moment I saw stars.

Buddy Bearpaw rolled on the ground. He screamed and clutched his right side. I'd hit him in the liver.

"Dad?" I crawled over to where Dad lay and put his head in my lap. "Wake up, Dad," I said. "It's all over. We can go home now."

Uncle Al came over to me. His left arm hung loose at his side. A stream of blood poured from his shoulder. He reached down and lifted one of Dad's eye lids. The pupil was large and fixed. I quickly closed the lid.

Uncle Al put his hand on my head. "Cry, Davy," he said. "Cry, hard!"

I turned my face. The tears came big and hot. I was sobbing.

Buddy Bearpaw was still screaming. Uncle Al went toward the cabin. I heard a shot, but didn't look up. Buddy Bearpaw quit screaming.

After awhile Uncle Al came out of the cabin holding Billy in his right arm. Billy looked like he was sleeping only he was real white and there was a big hole in his chest. Uncle Al was holding his cheek against Billy's face.

The command vehicle came rumbling down the road. Pete Marley stood in the turret pointing a shotgun at Uncle Al.

CHAPTER XV

The Marshall had a radio in the M-577 and in seconds a dozen police cars with sirens blaring and guns sticking out all over came down our road.

Pete Marley took Billy out of Uncle Al's arms and I thought for a minute he'd have to fight Uncle Al to do the job, but then Uncle Al let Billy go and turned around while Marley handcuffed him and led him to a car. "You take the other one," Marley hollered to Turk.

Turk came over to where I sat and jerked me up by the hair, then pushed me against a car. I'd seen guys frisked on television so I leaned forward like I thought I should while the deputy marshall ran his fingers along my body.

After that was over, he jerked my arms around behind me and put on handcuffs. The cuffs bit into my skin and I flinched. The flinching was a mistake cause the deputy laughed and squeezed the cuffs tighter.

Phil Snooper must have come up with the first car. He

was running everywhere taking pictures, mostly of the Indians. I didn't see him take any pictures of Dad or Billy. He came up and shoved his Hasselblad in my face, but the marshall pushed me into the car at that time so Snooper didn't get his pictures. He cursed Turk's back, then went to take another picture of Harry Echo.

I was in the back seat of a car with a deputy named Nate on one side and Turk on the other. "Better read him his rights," said Nate.

"All right," said Turk. "Listen, kid, these are your rights under the Miranda rule. You have a right to remain silent. You have the right to have an attorney. If you can't afford an attorney, one will be provided for you. You can have an attorney present when you answer any questions." Turk turned to Nate. "That all of them?"

"That's about it," said Nate. I got the impression they didn't read these rights too often.

"All right, kid. Now let's hear it!" Turk jerked me by the shoulder to face him. The handcuffs cut my wrists, but I didn't let on anything. I'd learned my lesson.

"Why'd you go poking your nose in this?" Turk prodded me when I was slow to answer.

I didn't say anything. If my right was to remain silent, then I figured I'd remain silent.

This made Turk mad, and he jerked me around quite a bit, but that only made me more determined not to say anything even if he pulled my tongue out.

We went through town with the sirens on. I looked out when we turned the corner at Main and Center. We were near the sidewalk and I looked straight into the faces of Steely Marks and his mother.

When she recognized me, Mrs. Marks' hand went to her mouth, and she jerked Steely back. It made me smile. So much for the good people of Pocatello, I thought.

The police car pulled into the garage behind the county jail. The radio had been going from the minute we left the ranch and there was a crowd in the garage when we arrived. Abe Solomon, the sheriff, was in charge.

Turk pulled me out of the car by the hair and I saw the

sheriff's mouth sort of tighten at the edge. "That's all for you," he said to Turk. "Take your cuffs off. It's our show now!"

Turk took his handcuffs off, but for a minute I didn't know my hands were free cause they still hurt. Then I brought them around in front of me. My wrists were bleeding and I wanted to rub them, but didn't know if I'd be allowed, so just left them hanging free.

"Where's the other one?" asked Abe Solomon.

Turk was surprised. "I thought they were ahead of us." Then he half laughed. "The hospital, I guess. The guy was wounded."

Abe Solomon grit his teeth and shook his head.

The sheriff took my shoulder and led me inside. He let me walk natural and didn't shove or push me like Turk had.

There's a room where they book you, but they had a drunk in there, and although the deputy was hurrying to get him booked, the drunk couldn't understand anything and kept falling down, so I was put into the drunk tank across the hall.

There was nothing to the drunk tank, just high steel walls and a cement floor. No windows or nothing else. Except for me, the place was empty.

In the door was a peep hole and I could tell that people kept looking at me. I didn't try to look back or anything, just leaned against the wall and rubbed my wrists.

In a few minutes the door opened and Abe Solomon motioned me out. He took me into the "booking room."

"Take off your clothes," said a deputy.

I took off my clothes. It made me smile. There's another good reason for having clean underwear. Besides being in an accident, you also might be arrested.

When I was naked, the deputy went through my wallet. I had two dollars and a card for the Y.M.C.A. The deputy counted the money, then took my wallet and clothes and locked them up. "Put on your underwear and socks," he said. Then he gave me a pair of white coveralls. They didn't fit; were real baggy.

After that he handed me a yellow piece of paper to fill

117

out with my name, age, and all that stuff. I pushed it back. I figured my rights covered that too.

The deputy started to argue but Abe Solomon who had been watching grinned and shook his head. "It's all right," he said and took me out.

The sheriff took me up in an elevator to the second floor. There a guy handed me a foam rubber mattress, one blanket, and a tin cup. After that they led me into the cell.

The cell was painted grey. The floor, the walls, everything grey. There were two other guys in there but I didn't pay them any attention. Near a corner I saw an empty bunk, so put my mattress on it and flopped down with the blanket over my head. There in the dark, under the blanket, everything came rushing in on me—Dad, Billy, jail, everything. I felt cold and alone, and very scared. After awhile I slept.

Someone was shaking my shoulder. I pulled the blanket down and saw it was one of the other guys in the cell. He was a little greasy haired guy with yellow teeth. He kept one hand inside his coveralls playing pocket pool.

"What do you want?" I asked.

"Food," he said. They'd pushed three trays, each with one spoon, through a slit in the wall.

"I don't want any," I tried to pull the blanket back over my head but the little guy wouldn't let me.

"Can I have it?" He leaned close to me.

"Sure." Anything to get his foul breath out of my face.

After awhile I heard the metal trays go back through the wall and the guy who had eaten my food came and sat on the edge of my bunk.

"My name's Dink," he said. "I'm in for snatching cars." He stuck out his chest proudly. "That's my profession. Snatching cars!"

I sat up on the bunk and pulled my knees under my chin. "What do they call a guy who snatches cars?" I asked.

The other guy in the cell, a tall, good looking Mexican about my size came over. "They call 'em a thief!" He said.

I laughed along with the Mexican. Dink didn't think that it was funny.

"I'm Carlos," said the Mexican. "I'm a manufacturer."

"And what's that?" I asked.

"I grow stuff, grass. You know, marijuana."

"You can't grow much stuff here," I said.

"No, but I used to," said Carlos. "Worked on a farm north of town. The farmer raised corn and between the rows of corn I grew grass. Did pretty good too, before I made a mistake."

"What was the mistake?"

"Befriending a Texas Mexican," said Carlos. "Met the guy in a bar and he seemed okay, so I took him in. Bad mistake!" Carlos sighed and looked at the floor. "The guy turned out to be a State Narc Agent. Never trust a Texas Mexican," was Carlos' advice. "You can never figure them."

"What's with you?" Dink had both hands in his coveralls playing pocket pool.

"What with what?" I asked.

"What're you in for?" asked Dink.

"They caught me playing cowboys and Indians." I thought it would be funny and at first Dink and Carlos laughed, but then they got to figuring who I was. Dink sucked in his breath.

"Jesus, so you're the one!" In the space between the bars and the windows called the catwalk where the deputies came to check on the prisoners they had a television set. It had been on the boob tube.

"Can't figure 'em!" Carlos looked down at me, then he and Dink both left me alone. They'd seen enough bodies on the tube to be impressed. I felt sort of freakish about it, but couldn't do anything. I didn't look at the television.

CHAPTER XVI

At 2:30 p.m. Abe Solomon came to get me. "Time for your arraignment," he said.

I didn't know what an arraignment was, but got up from my cot without saying anything and followed him out.

"Pretty fancy," chided Dink. "For his arraignment, the Indian fighter gets the big man himself. Me? I only get a deputy."

"Shut up Dink!" Abe Solomon said. Dink shut up.

The sheriff pushed the elevator button. While we waited, he looked me up and down. I shifted nervously in the baggy coveralls. Abe Solomon, satisfied that his charge was holding up okay, took me by the arm and led me into the elevator. My arm felt like it was gripped in a vise, only Abe Solomon didn't squeeze. Just held me firm without hurting. "You going to give me any trouble?" He asked.

I shook my head.

"That's smart," he said and let go of my arm.

We took the elevator down to the basement, and from there through a tunnel over to the courthouse. The tunnel had steam pipes running along its ceiling. The sheriff had to watch his head so he didn't bump it on a valve.

There was an elevator at the end of the tunnel, but we didn't take it. Instead we went up a flight of stairs to a room marked "Magistrate Court. Room One."

Magistrate Court One wasn't as big as the District Court we visited in Civics Class. For one thing it was smaller and there wasn't any place for a jury.

There were two tables with chairs in front of the raised seat where the judge sat. Our Civics Class was told that the judge's seat is called the woolsack.

Then there was a small rail and a place for spectators to sit. Only no spectators had been allowed to attend.

A big guy who looked like a policeman, only he was the bailiff, sat on one side of the woolsack, and on the other side was a woman secretary.

Carl Bailey, who was the District Attorney for Bannock County, sat at one table with two assistants. Carl Bailey was a medium sized guy who was only about thirty, but bleached his hair white so he'd look older. He came to Pocatello from Wyoming about four years earlier and as soon as he hit town started hollering about how much corruption there was in the district attorney's office and how the people ought to elect someone new, like Carl Bailey.

Well, Carl Bailey got elected and after it was over no one could see as how there was any difference in the District Attorney's Office, because the same people were still there only a new chief. Now Carl Bailey was hollering about how much corruption there was in the State Attorney General's Office.

Uncle Al sat at the other table with Pete Marley. I went over and sat down next to Uncle Al.

"Hi there, Davy boy," said Uncle Al. Uncle Al looked like he'd aged a hundred years since I'd seen him that morning. Pete Marley jabbed him with his elbow to keep him quiet, but Uncle Al wouldn't keep quiet. "Hang in there Davy." He tried to jab Pete Marley back but couldn't as his hands were cuffed to his sides.

I put my hand on Uncle Al's shoulder. He winced as if I'd hurt him. I saw then that his shoulder was bandaged. "Keep your hands down," snarled Pete Marley.

Abe Solomon didn't say anything, but he looked a lot at Uncle Al and then Pete Marley and I could tell the sheriff was mad about something.

The bailiff got up. "All please rise. Magistrate Fifth District Court in session. Honorable William Fishkin presiding," the bailiff announced.

We got to our feet. Uncle Al had trouble, so Pete Marley jerked him up. Uncle Al winced, then tried to grin at me.

The judge came in and sat down. "Please be seated," he said. Judge William Fishkin was a short, mostly bald man, in his sixties. He wore thick glasses, and studied the papers on his desk a long time before saying anything, then he looked down at our table. "David McGrath?" He asked.

I started to rise, but the judge waved me down. "Albert McGrath?" Uncle Al nodded, but didn't try to get up.

"David and Albert McGrath," said the Judge. "You have been charged with five counts of murder in the first degree. The maximum penalty in Idaho for this crime is death by hanging."

Carl Bailey nodded with satisfaction. This was the most murders he'd ever had.

I felt strange. Nothing seemed real. Abe Solomon put his hand on my arm. Uncle Al pursed his lips and stared at the table.

Judge Fishkin kept talking. "You have a right to enter a plea at this time," he said. "You have a right to a trial by jury. You have a right to be represented by an attorney. If you are in need, the court will appoint an attorney for you. You have a right to have witnesses subpoenaed for you. You have a right to remain silent or to testify in your own behalf. If you elect to testify, you are subject to cross examination."

The Judge said a lot more things, but I was real dizzy and didn't understand him.

I heard Uncle Al say "not guilty."

Then there was talk about a lawyer and Carl Bailey said something about Aaron Creech. And they talked about me being a juvenile and the District Attorney said, "I'll discuss that with Aaron Creech prior to the Preliminary Hearing tomorrow at 10:00 a.m." Then it was over and Judge Fishkin went out.

Uncle Al went out with Pete Marley and Turk. The sheriff sat with me for awhile, then we got up and left the court room.

We went back through the tunnel to the jail. I was walking pretty wobbly so the sheriff took me to the back door. "Take a few deep breaths Davy," said Abe Solomon.

I took the breaths and felt better. The sun was shining warm on the asphalt of the parking lot. To the west were the mountains, and then farther south, the ranch. There are lots of arroyas and aspen draws up there where a guy could hide, I thought. In half a dozen bounds I could be down the steps and through the parking lot. In ten minutes I could be across town and into the foothills. Abe Solomon would not be able to catch me, I knew. No one could catch me!

Then I saw the Judge standing on top of a prowl car. He shook his head. "No, Davy," he said.

"Feel better?" asked the sheriff. He stood a couple of paces behind me.

"Yes," I said, and turned back into the jail. Abe Solomon grinned.

CHAPTER XVII

Someone passed the trays through the wall about 4:00 p.m. They had ham, and lima beans, corn bread and coffee. This time I was hungry. I ate everything and drank the coffee. Mom would be angry at me for drinking the coffee, I thought.

Dink and Carlos made it plain they didn't want to talk to me, so I lay on my bunk. After the trays went back through the wall, I heard someone call my name.

Out on the catwalk was the sheriff with Phil Snooper; Snooper and the four thousand dollar Hasselblad. "Hey McGrath, come here!" he said.

I laid on the bunk and pretended not to hear.

"Make him come here and talk to me," Snuder complained to the sheriff.

"Nope," said Abe Solomon. "Can't make him say one word." He was sort of laughing.

"Then I'm going in there," said Snuder. "I'll make him talk."

I stiffened but still gave him the silent rasberry. I could fix that Snooper good before the sheriff got me off.

Abe Solomon shook his head. I guess he knew what was going through my mind. "No, Snuder, you're not going anywhere. I shouldn't have let you in here."

"Hey mister, take my picture. I'm a real bad one!" Dink came over to the bars in front of Snuder.

"What'd you do?" Snuder was interested.

"I raped my mother!" At first Dink was serious, then couldn't hold it and burst out laughing. Carlos laughed along with him. The sheriff smiled.

Snuder got all red and left the catwalk. Abe Solomon opened the window a little wider at Dink's request, then went out. I heard the heavy metal door slam shut.

A little while after that, they let Mom come up. She wasn't allowed on the catwalk, and had to look at me through the thick glass panel in the door which was about as big as the palm of my hand. Below the glass was a metal screen which you talk through.

Mom was wearing a green pantsuit outfit with a white blouse that Dad had gotten her for her birthday. Her birthday is in August. She is a Leo. Dad was an Aries, and I guess that's why they got along well together.

"How are you, Davy?" Mom asked. Her eyes went over me the best she could through the little window. I could tell she didn't approve of the ill fitting coveralls.

"Fine Mom," I said. "Just fine!" I tried to smile.

"They took Frank and Billy to Dunning's Mortuary." She bit her lip and tried hard not to cry.

"That's nice," I lied. "Mr. Dunning is a good man."

"Davy, tomorrow morning at ten is the preliminary hearing and the sheriff suggested I bring you some clean clothes. They have them downstairs." The words gushed out. She was wound tight to keep from breaking up and had rehearsed what she was going to say.

"What's the preliminary hearing?" I asked.

"From what Mr. Solomon says, I guess it's where they charge you and bind you over for trial."

"Did Mr. Solomon say what the charge was?" I'd heard it at the arraignment, but hoped I was dreaming.

"Murder," said Mom. Now she was crying. Big tears pushed out the corners of her eyes. "Carl Bailey has been on television all afternoon. He says what you and Al did was murder, and he wants you tried as an adult and he wants you both to hang." She buried her face in her hands.

"He would," I said.

"What's that?" She lifted her head to catch my words.

"He would like to see us hang," I said. "Mr. Ravelli told me that Carl Bailey wants to be Attorney General, and I guess he figures this is his big step up. Have you seen Uncle Al?" I asked.

"No. I asked the sheriff to see him, but Mr. Solomon said Al wasn't in his jail, but was over at the hospital. Oh! And I've got good news." Mom managed a smile. "Mr. Creech called."

"What did he want?" I didn't know if this was good news or not.

"He said he was sorry to hear about the trouble you were in and wanted to know if he could do anything."

"Like what?"

"Maybe standing up for you at the preliminary hearing." Mom looked at me expectantly. Maybe this was good news.

"Did he say what it would cost?" I asked.

"Somehow that did come up," Mom said. "Mr. Creech said that matters like this were very expensive."

"How expensive?"

"I told him I had two thousand dollars in savings, but Mr. Creech said that wasn't near enough. He said if he had his way he'd like to take the case for nothing but he didn't think the bar association and the other attorneys would allow that." Mom acted evasive.

"So then what?" I caught myself shouting and looked around to see Carlos and Dink listening.

"Mr. Creech thinks it would be best if I signed the ranch

over to him until this business is settled." Mom didn't look at me.

"You didn't do it?" I felt like a knife was sticking in my gut ready to slice up.

"Not yet," she said. "I'm to call him back tonight. I wanted to talk to you first. You know you're the man of the house now, Davy." Mom gave me a hopeful smile. I felt the knife ease out.

"Wait until after the preliminary," I said. "Then we'll see what happens. Besides, there are other lawyers."

"Okay," she said. "By the way, Paul De Gamma called and said he was also coming to the preliminary."

"Won't let him in," I said. "Closed, like the arraignment."

A deputy came up to let Mom know that she had better go.

"Mom?" Now it was my turn for the tears to well up, but I brushed my fists across my lids so nothing showed. "Did I do wrong?" I asked.

"No, Davy," she said. "You did just right. Dad would have said 'You're no slouch!' "

She followed the deputy to the elevator and the door closed behind them.

A toilet occupied a corner of the cell—no cubicle, no curtains, nothing but a toilet sitting right out in front of God and everybody. I hadn't been to the bathroom since I was put in the cell. As a consequence, I was mighty uncomfortable.

Dink had used the facilities on two occasions and Carlos once. The fact that it all hung out for everyone to see didn't bother them at all. With me it was different. I was embarrassed.

Finally I had the choice of either doing it on the throne or in my pants. I chose the throne. Even at that, I tried to be as quiet as possible.

I'd been seated only ten seconds when the cell door opened and Abe Solomon came in with Pete Marley. The marshall didn't look too good. I could tell something was eating him. It looked like he'd been arguing with the sheriff.

The marshall's little pig eyes took in everything in the

cell; paused for a moment on Dink and Carlos then came to rest on me. He stayed near the door. "Hey, kid, come here!" he said.

Dink laughed. "Davy sure gets a lot of company," he said. "And it's always the same. 'Hey kid, come here!'"

Marley glared at Dink and took a step into the cell. Dink shut up and pretended to become interested in the television, I sat on the throne and made out like that was the only spot in the world.

"McGrath come here!" I could feel Marley's gaze hard on my neck, but didn't turn. Right then I farted. Nothing planned, it just came out. Dink and Carlos snickered. Marley cursed. "You little bastard!"

He took a step toward me, but Abe Solomon stopped him. "Not in my lockup, you don't!" The sheriff jerked the marshall back by the arm.

Pete Marley doubled his fist like he wanted to fight, then backed off. "Let's get out of here," he said.

They went out the door and I finished what I was doing on the throne.

That night I thought about Uncle Al and a lot of other things. For the first time, I prayed before going to bed.

CHAPTER XVIII

In the morning at a quarter to seven, a trustee shoved breakfast trays through the slit in the wall. Dink was there to get them. I laid on my cot with my eyes closed. I didn't care if I ate or not.

"Breakfast," said Dink. He hovered over my tray, giving his snaggle-toothed smile, hoping I'd pass up the meal.

"Thanks." I swung my legs over the side of the cot and snapped a coverall button that had come loose during the night.

Dink set my tray on an empty bunk, then backed sullenly away. I laughed. Dink was a funny little rat. Transparent as hell.

It was a good breakfast; scrambled eggs, bacon, toast and jelly. I was hungrier than I thought. I ate everything. I looked at the coffee, thought about Mom, then drank it all.

I shouldn't have done it, I thought. I could get in trouble. That was funny. I laughed.

Dink and Carlos looked at me and moved closer together. They figured the crazy Indian fighter was going off his rocker again. That was funny too, so I laughed some more.

I put my tray near the slot in the wall. When the trustee came around, Dink could pass it through.

The television was blaring; more pictures; more talk. The massacre on Jimmy Creek, they called it. I lay on my cot and stared at the ceiling. Dink and Carlos watched television. From time to time I caught them glancing at me, then whispering together. I didn't care.

At 9:00 a.m., Abe Solomon came in with some clothes. "Put these on for your preliminary," he said.

Mom had sent clean underwear and socks. My best white shirt, and blue slacks. I took off the coveralls and threw them on the cot, then hesitated about my shorts. I wasn't used to undressing before strangers.

The sheriff sensing my embarrassment, looked away. Dink and Carlos snickered. I took off my shorts and threw them on top of the coveralls. Dink looked real close. I ignored him and put on clean clothes. They felt good.

I followed Abe Solomon out of the cell and got into the elevator. "You gonna give me any trouble?" asked the sheriff.

I shook my head.

"Good!" He said.

We went to the basement, then through the tunnel to the courthouse. This time we took the elevator to the third floor. "Magistrate Court. Room Three," read the sign on the door. We went in.

This was a smaller room than where I'd had my arraignment. Along the west wall was a six man jury box, then in front the Judge's woolsack, and seats on either side for the secretary and witness.

In front of the woolsack were two tables, then a small rail and two rows of gallery seats.

The room wasn't empty. At the prosecution table was

Carl Bailey and his two assistants. They were talking and laughing.

When I came in they looked at me, grinned then went back to their talking. I lifted my chin and straightened my shoulders. They didn't like that.

"Sit here, Davy." Abe Solomon steered me to the empty defense table.

A few minutes later, Pete Marley and Turk came in with Uncle Al. Uncle Al's wrists were handcuffed behind him and he looked bad. He was still wearing the clothes he was arrested in—green flannel shirt and brown slacks. Only his clothes were wrinkled.

Uncle Al seemed real tired, but still gave me a smile. Pete Marley took the handcuffs off him and led him over to my table and pushed him into a chair beside me. After that Aaron Creech came in and sat next to Uncle Al.

Pete Marley and Turk went to stand near the wall.

The bailiff came into the room and stood beside the woolsack. "All please rise," he said. We stood up.

The Honorable Herbert A. Wendell followed by a secretary, came into the room and sat on the woolsack. "Please be seated," he said.

Judge Herbert A. Wendell was a medium sized man who bent toward the thin side, only I couldn't tell for sure because of the black robe he wore. He had quite a bit of black hair that he wore short so people couldn't see how grey he was getting. I guessed he was about the same age as Dad.

He had a boy named Herb Junior who was a year older than me. Herb Junior was a quiet kid about my size. He had red hair too.

Herb Junior was on the track team, but I never got to know him too well, him being a sprinter and me a miler. But I guess he was all right; least ways he never leaned on me, and I never leaned on him.

"Preliminary hearing number 12758 is now in session," said the judge. "The State of Idaho versus Albert McGrath and David McGrath, a minor." He leaned forward and looked down at Uncle Al and me. "You are charged with five counts of murder in the first degree."

I felt cold and prickly all over, but stared at the floor. It was dumb but I thought that after the preliminary they'd take us out and hang us, and I had forgot to tell Mom that Dad wanted to be buried in the draw above the orchard. Maybe I could shout it out from the scaffold where we would be hanged and somebody would hear me and tell Mom.

"Mr. Prosecutor," Judge Wendell looked at Carl Bailey. Carl Bailey nodded.

"The council for the defense," the judge looked at Aaron Creech. Aaron Creech smiled and nodded at the judge. "Please proceed," said Judge Wendell.

Carl Bailey got to his feet. His silver hair combed straight back like a lion's mane. He looked like one of those lawyers on the television shows. He wore a dark blue suit and smiled a lot. "Your Honor," he said. "This won't take long. I know how busy you are."

"Take as long as necessary. This is a murder case and I'm not busy!" snapped the Judge. It was plain that he didn't like Carl Bailey.

Carl Bailey quit smiling and looked at the table nervously. His assistant pushed a stack of papers at him. The prosecutor glanced at the papers, then picked them up and walked over and laid them before the judge. He then went back behind his table.

"We are all aware of the deaths of five, fine Americans on Jimmy Creek yesterday," he said. "Before you I have placed the pathologist's preliminary report. The deceased were slain by bullets from a 7 MM Remington 30-06 and a 300 Savage. Weapons registered in the name of Albert McGrath and Frank McGrath.

The prosecutor smiled, threw his arm back and passed a hand over his mane of silver hair. The judge glanced cursorly at the papers laid before him. Aaron Creech leaned toward Uncle Al and whispered something that I couldn't hear. Uncle Al nodded but didn't say anything.

"Do you have more evidence to present, Mr. Prosecutor?" asked the judge. He spoke harshly.

"Not at this time," said the Prosecutor.

Judge Wendell turned to Aaron Creech. "Does the defense wish to offer evidence at this time?" he asked.

Aaron Creech talked to Uncle Al a long time then stood up.

"We waive that right, your Honor," he said.

"What about this boy?" asked Judge Wendell. "He has a right to be tried as a juvenile."

"We waive that too, your Honor," said Aaron Creech.

Judge Wendell pursed his lips. He wasn't satisfied. He looked at Carl Bailey, then at Aaron Creech. "Mr. Creech," he said. "Do your clients know what it means to waive their right to present evidence? That they will be bound over to stand trial in Fifth District Court on five counts of murder?"

Aaron Creech looked at Uncle Al. Uncle Al nodded.

"My clients realize this," said Aaron Creech. "In their best interest, it is felt prudent not to present evidence at this time." He smiled and patted me on the shoulder.

"Davy?" said Judge Wendell. "Do you understand what's going on?"

I stood up but stayed on my right to remain silent and looked at the floor without saying anything.

"Davy McGrath!" The Judge sounded mad, like my Dad sometimes. "Look at me!" I looked at the Judge. He didn't seem mad, only hurt. "Tell me what happened."

I tried to stay on my rights, but couldn't. "They killed Billy," I blurted out. "Dad was going to give them the ranch, and he called up Phil Snuder and told him the Indians could have the ranch if they'd let Billy go. Phil Snuder said to wait till morning, so we did. But that night Zane Bodkins came and said they'd killed Billy."

I guess I was talking a lot and once Aaron Creech was going to stop me, but didn't.

"Then we went up there," I said. "We were plenty mad, but Dad, he cools off real fast and when Russell Jones came out with a white flag, Dad went to talk to him and they shot Dad. After that they came out and we let them have it." I quit talking. I'd made a fool of myself. I sat down.

Carl Bailey looked sheepish. Aaron Creech looked at Uncle Al and shrugged as if he didn't know what I said was good or not.

"What about these?" Judge Wendell picked up the stack of pathology reports. "Are there reports here on Billy and Frank McGrath?"

"No." Carl Bailey got red. "I didn't think it necessary."

"Well, it is necessary," said the Judge. "Do you have a report on Billy McGrath?"

The Prosecutor's Assistant shoved a piece of paper toward Carl Bailey. "Yes, I do," admitted the prosecutor.

"How did the boy die?" The Judge leaned forward.

"He was shot." Carl Bailey pretended to read from the paper.

"When?" snapped the Judge. "How near to the others?"

"Ten hours before." The prosecutor started to chew on the paper. The assistant pulled it away.

"And what about you?" The Judge turned on Aaron Creech. "Does the defense attorney have any questions to ask?"

"Why yes, I do."

"Like what?"

Aaron Creech came alive. "Is the United States Marshall here?" he asked.

Pete Marley stepped away from the wall.

"Did you see the shooting at the cabin on Jimmy Creek?" asked Aaron Creech.

"No sir!" said Pete Marley. He stood at attention. Real proud!

"Did you hear the shooting?"

"Yes." Pete Marley acted less confident. He glanced at Carl Bailey.

"What kind of fire did you hear?" asked Aaron Creech.

"High powered rifles," said Pete Marley. He let his voice trail.

"And?" added the lawyer.

"And automatic weapons," admitted Pete Marley.

"Which weapons did you hear first?" asked Aaron Creech.

Pete Marley looked at Carl Bailey. The prosecutor refused to meet his gaze.

"Answer me, Mr. Marley!" demanded Aaron Creech. "What weapons did you hear first?"

"The automatic weapons." Pete Marley clenched the handcuffs at his side.

"And who had the automatic weapons?" Aaron Creech rocked confidently on his heels.

"The Indians," said Pete Marley.

Judge Wendell had followed the questioning closely. He waved Pete Marley back against the wall, then sat for several minutes with his eyes closed.

"Is there any more, gentlemen?" He looked at Carl Bailey.

"No," said Carl Bailey. "I believe the State has demonstrated probable cause."

Aaron Creech whispered to Uncle Al a minute, then said. "No more evidence your Honor."

"Davy," said the Judge. "Please stand."

I stood up.

"The reason for a preliminary hearing, Davy," said Judge Wendell, "is to establish probable cause that a crime has been committed. And if it's decided there is probable cause a crime has been committed, then evidence has to be presented showing that the defendant, in this case you and your Uncle Al, committed the crime." The judge looked at me. I tried to look back but couldn't meet his eyes.

"Davy," said the judge. "You and your Uncle Al can go home."

"What?" Carl Bailey jumped to his feet.

"The defendants are dismissed," said the judge. "I refuse to bind them over."

"But five Native Americans are dead," protested the prosecuting attorney. "This case can't be over."

"You're wrong on one account," said the judge. "Seven Native Americans are dead. The McGraths were also born

137

in this country. But the case is certainly not over. I'm going to investigate this matter thoroughly."

I looked up at the judge, then at Uncle Al and started to leave the courtroom. Aaron Creech came over wanting to shake my hand but I turned my back and left the room.

Carl Bailey and his assistants were at their table shuffling papers. "Wait'll he gets outside," I heard Carl Bailey say. "They'll get the little bastard."

CHAPTER XIV

It's not easy to find your way out of the Bannock County Courthouse, particularly if you've been coming in through the back tunnel. I wasn't sure which way to go, but there were some stairs nearby, so I took them. On the second floor a sign with an arrow attested to the fact that the Drivers License Office had moved to the basement. I turned the opposite direction from the arrow, then had to wait a few minutes for Uncle Al to catch up.

We went down another half flight of stairs, and were outside the courthouse.

A crowd stood out front on the lawn. Someone had knocked over the "Keep off the Grass" sign. Most of the people were Indians or from the university. In back I could see Mom, but she couldn't get near.

When we came out on the steps, most everyone started shouting and shaking their fists. Phil Snooper was down there taking pictures.

A couple of men were talking to each other and not paying any attention to the racket. Phil Snooper stuck his head in front of them and pointed at me. These men too started shouting, and Phil Snooper took their picture.

I was going to go down the steps toward Mom, but the Indian men blocked the sidewalk. Someone shouted, "Let's get the son-of-a-bitch," and the crowd started coming at me and Uncle Al.

Closest to me I could see my former friend, Andy Echo, and there behind him was Lance Buckner, the movie star. Lance Buckner was screaming and jumping around.

For a few seconds, I didn't know what to do. I thought about ducking back inside the courthouse. That would have been easy.

Then I got to figuring I'd be meeting these people all my life and it wouldn't be any good to always be ducking around. I looked at Uncle Al. He grinned and winked at me. And all of a sudden the whole thing seemed sort of funny and I started to laugh and walked down the steps swinging.

Andy Echo threw a punch at me, but it didn't amount to anything, so I let him have it. I got him good, I know that, because I felt it go into my shoulder and felt bones break in his face as he went down. Then I got Lance Buckner. That didn't feel like anything.

After that I don't know what happened. I was swinging wild, and missing a lot, but I was hitting some too because I could hear men grunt. Little lights kept going off in my head, so I knew I was getting it too, and then everything started getting black and then I wasn't getting hit anymore and it started to get light.

I hadn't seen him come up, but when I raised my head, I saw Paul De Gamma and there were a lot more guys from the steel car shop that had driven up in a yellow railroad truck. The guys with Paul De Gamma all carried little green wrecking bars that have a blunted point on one end.

The railroad guys didn't hit anyone, only the Indians knew they would if they had too, so the Indians all got out of the way and let Mom and Paul De Gamma come toward me and Uncle Al.

Mom grabbed hold of me like she hadn't seen me in years and was hugging me and crying a lot. Only it was a different kind of crying from before, like she was real happy.

Phil Snooper came crowding up and pushed his Hasselblad in our face. Mom got mad at that, and before Phil Snooper could back away she snatched the camera and threw it over her head.

Phil Snooper cussed Mom and went for the Hasselblad but before he could get it an Indian guy had stepped on it and then another did the same thing.

Phil Snooper then turned on the Indians and called them "stupid savages." The Indian guys hadn't meant to step on the camera, but when Phil Snooper took to calling them names, they got mad and smashed the Hasselblad real good, and smashed the photographer's fingers when he reached around their feet.

Paul De Gamma wanted to pick me up, but I wouldn't let him. So he took my hand, and seeing that Uncle Al was following led us out of the crowd toward Mom's gas guzzler.

Mom was still crying and holding on to me, and was wiping my face with her hankie. But I said she didn't need to because I was all right. My words sounded funny, cause my lips had swollen up from getting punched. I laughed and then Paul De Gamma and the Steel Car Shop guys started laughing too. The Indians looked at us sort of funny like, then drifted away.

Paul De Gamma told his assistant foreman to take the men back to work, then he got in Mom's gas guzzler with us.

We drove to Dunning's Mortuary where they'd taken Dad and Billy. "We've come for the bodies of Frank and Billy McGrath," I told Mr. Dunning.

The mortician was surprised at my request. "No one has ever done that before," he said. "Where do you intend to take the bodies?"

"Up to the ranch to be buried," I said.

"You can't do that," he said. "There are laws about where people can be buried, and they have to be embalmed and a lot of things."

I just looked at the guy and could tell he was real scared; him knowing who I was and me being so ugly from getting beat up.

Still jabbering about laws he went and got Dad's and Billy's bodies and brought them out on a guerney covered by a sheet and helped us load them in the gas guzzler. So I guess there really wasn't so many laws about being buried after all.

We stopped at the house for a few things, then drove up to the ranch. The ground was soft, but Mom got the station wagon up to the top of the orchard where Dad had told me he wanted to be buried.

It took me two hours to dig Dad and Billy's grave. Paul De Gamma wanted to help but I wouldn't let him. Because while I was digging I got to thinking and began to understand a lot of things. I realized how it had been between Dad and Porky.

Porky had been Dad's dog. He'd had him even before I was born. Dad and Porky hunted and fished together and were about as close as a man and dog can be. Then Porky got old. Seemed like it happened all of a sudden. It was winter and cold, and Dad wanted to take Porky inside but the Lab wouldn't have it, but when he got outside he fell down and couldn't get up and cried because his legs hurt, so Dad took him out one day and shot him.

I knew as I dug that there are some things a man has to do by himself for his friend. And I knew that sometimes it was like having your guts ripped out, but you have to do them anyway.

When I'd finished with the grave, Mom handed me her purple quilt and I put it in the bottom. Uncle Al was starting to feel a little better, but still couldn't raise his arm, so Paul De Gamma handed me down first Dad, and then Billy. I put Billy's head on Dad's shoulder. Then I guess I did a stupid thing. Before I closed the quilt over them, I put in a deck of cards and a cribbage board.

I placed some boards over the quilt, and then we all dropped a few handfuls of dirt in the hole, then I started to fill it up.

After a while I saw that Mom looked awful tired. "Mom," I said. "I'm pretty hungry. We got anything to eat in the cabin?"

"I'll go down and see while you're finishing up," she said. I could tell she liked the idea.

Paul De Gamma protested. "I'll buy some food," he said.

Mom wouldn't hear of it. She needed to make something, so finally everyone agreed.

"Don't wait for me," I said to Paul and Uncle Al. "I'll be done here in a minute, and I'd sort of like to walk down alone."

Uncle Al and Paul De Gamma acted like they wanted to argue with me, but didn't and got in the car with Mom and drove down through the orchard.

I figured I was done and ready to walk down when I saw the Judge and Dad watching me. First time I'd ever seen the Judge wear clothes. Dad was shaking his head and pointing at the grave. I looked again and noticed I hadn't replaced the sod. I put the sod around as good as I could and Dad seemed pleased.

To one side, I saw Billy fooling with that Tiberius bull. The Judge didn't like having the bull around, and to tell the truth neither did I.